CW00847359

Black Jack Justice

by Gregg Taylor

ISBN: 1466290862
ISBN-13: 978-1466290860

For Clarissa, Max and Tess
Who slept while I wrote this

Chapter One

The name is Justice. Jack Justice.

The life of a private detective lends itself to a certain amount of introspection. You live far enough outside the shop-worn clichés of day-to-day living that you never quite feel like a part of the world at large, yet you are forced to be a keen observer of it. And as you observe, you can't help but notice some of the more unpleasant proclivities of that nice, normal society that goes about its business outside your door every day pretending that it doesn't have a dirty little secret. But it does. They all do. And when it all goes wrong, that is when they come to see me.

Sadly, while the life of a detective lends itself to this sort of deep thought, the men who choose this line of work are generally pretty poorly suited to such meditation. At no point in my illustrious academic career did I flip a coin to choose between detective work and philosophy, and there are some pretty compelling reasons why that is true. So although my perch offers me a unique opportunity to analyze the human condition and the great truths that bind us all, I am frequently disappointed by how often those observations take the form of something that your mother always told you, and her mother before that.

Today that truth seemed to be, "It's always calm before the storm". The dull patter of largely disinterested rain against the windows, the soothing rattle of the coffee percolator, the radiator just beginning to sing – together they were a quiet symphony of comfort. And further to that comfort, there was a small, mousey man sitting in the client chair, which though it might mean trouble also meant rent money, and this I found good.

"How do you take your coffee, Mr. Mayfield?" I asked him. He seemed startled by the question at first and smiled a little sheepishly at his own reaction. I had only asked because it seemed polite, and it might imply that there were options available to him. There was neither milk nor cream in the small icebox in the corner, which also had not held ice in over a year. There might have been sugar somewhere but I couldn't have sworn to it.

"Black is fine, thank you," Roger Mayfield said conveniently, glancing back toward Tom's empty desk to his left. Everyone did. A few years back I might have stopped to reassure him that my old partner was unlikely to come back and intrude upon our quiet conference, but I had mostly given that up. The letters on the door now read *Jack Justice Investigations*, and I didn't think it needed more explanation than that. One of these days I was going to have to get rid of that desk. If I could get a couple of bucks for it.

"Here you go," I said, handing him a cup of a new blend I was working on. I watched for a reaction. Sometimes the best way to judge a cup of coffee is by the effect it had upon others. Roger Mayfield took an absent-minded sip and did the smallest of double-takes, as if he had been pulled back to Earth from a considerable distance.

"That's awfully good," he blinked.

"Mostly Costa Rican," I said with an effort of modesty, "laced with some very dark varieties for texture on the palate."

"What?" Mayfield blinked again, and the moment was gone.

"What do you do, Mister Mayfield?" I asked, sitting behind my own desk and shifting a few papers as though I might start to take notes at any moment. The industrious gumshoe at work.

"I'm a City Planner," he said as if that explained everything.

"Cities have those?" I asked with surprise.

"Oh my, yes," Mayfield said, coming to life a little bit.

"Always seemed to me that they kind of just happened," I shrugged.

Mayfield smiled as if I were a dull but adorable child. "Well, even a few decades ago, Mr. Justice, that might have been true. But these days, particularly with the enormous investment of taxpayer dollars required to fund urban initiatives of any size, there needs to be thorough planning and development."

"The folks we elect don't do that?" I wasn't really that interested in what he did, but it seemed to be bringing him out of his shell a little.

Mayfield seemed amused. "Oh my, Mr. Justice, politicians do not really have the time, inclination or training for this kind of work. Some of these projects require vast amounts of preparation; they require a continuity that elected office does not always allow."

I may have raised an eyebrow. "So you make sure our city carries on being planned properly regardless of whom we vote for?"

"Yes," he beamed. He was pleased by this, and blissfully unaware of any irony.

"All right then," I said, leaning back in my chair. "So what brings a bright young man such as yourself into my office?"

He flushed a little, but did not seem displeased at the implication of youth and intelligence. Men who are truly possessed of neither quality rarely object to the suggestion that they hold both.

He was about five-eight, maybe five-nine. Forty-five years old if I was any judge, though he could have been older. Not much more than a hundred and thirty pounds soaking wet. His suit was neat, his tie was tied with a precision to which my own was thoroughly unaccustomed and his spectacles sat neatly in their place without drifting down the bridge of his nose. He looked like an accountant designed by a team of actuaries. There weren't a lot of things that could bring him to do something as exotic as hiring a detective. Had to be a frail in there somewhere.

"I… um…" His train of thought was boarding at the station, and he seemed to be unable to find the word that would start him down the track. He glanced at the empty desk again. Yeah, it was a frail. He didn't want to have to say this more than once. But he didn't have that hangdog expression, that defeated air of a man who wanted his own wife followed. Those were the worst. A man put in the shameful position of having to ask another man to help him prove himself a cuckold. And a stranger at that. I hated those meetings. It was like watching a film of a car wreck in slow motion. That wasn't Roger Mayfield, not today it wasn't anyway. So if he wasn't the *cheatee*, he had to be the *cheater*.

"What's her name?" I said with just the right amount of smile creeping across my face. Cheaters like to feel that their antics are adorable, and that other men are jealous of their virility. I had very little doubt that my virility could take Mayfield's out back by the bike racks and beat the living tar out of it, but I knew when to play my part.

Roger Mayfield flushed a little, and even stammered. "I… I'm sorry?"

"Come on, Mr. Mayfield," I said. "We're both men of the world, and whatever it is that you've been up to, I assure you that I've seen and heard a hundred times worse. Your detective is like your doctor. I can't help you if you stammer and blush. So what's her name?"

He blinked a few times, as if saying the words out loud went entirely against his programming. "Janet," he said at last. "Janet Timms."

"Nice name," I nodded.

"Yes," he said hesitantly.

"Nice girl?" I asked.

"Well… yes." His ears turned bright red. She must be a nice girl all right, but not in the way Ma Justice would have used the phrase.

"Tell me about it," I said.

"Mr. Justice, this is not really about Janet," he said.

"Then what is it about?"

"I'm very much afraid that I am being blackmailed," he said all at once, as if it were a breath he had been holding in for days.

We looked at one another for a moment.

"The activity which has provided the fodder for this blackmail," I asked without expression, "do you perform it with Janet?"

He turned crimson and stammered. "Well, yes," he said at last.

"Then it is a little bit about Janet, isn't it?" I asked.

He didn't seem to have anything to say about that, so I continued. "You see, Mr. Mayfield, a lot of people like to compartmentalize these things before they even sit down in that chair. But that isn't your job. That's what you pay me for. Right now everything has everything to do with everything, and I am the one person in the world from whom you do not need to protect your secrets."

"Yes," he said, sounding unconvinced.

"First of all, so I can use the correct nomenclature, is Janet '*Miss*' Timms?" I asked, pretending to make notes.

"What?" He seemed confused. "Oh, yes. Yes, she is."

"So the… complications… are entirely on your end?" I gave a glace toward the wedding band on his left hand to gently prompt him.

"Yes," he said quietly. "My wife Anne. She knows nothing."

"Of course," I said. "And has your blackmailer threatened to tell her, or has he got something to show?"

Mayfield shifted in his chair slightly. The blackmailer had something to show all right.

"I may have misspoken slightly, Mr. Justice," Mayfield began.

"Heaven forefend," I said quietly, mostly for my own amusement.

"I have not, as yet, received a specific threat of blackmail," he said, folding his hands as if that were the end of it.

"All right," I said, "what *have* you received? People don't just pull blackmail out of the clear blue sky."

He shifted in his seat again. "A photograph," he said at last.

We sat in silence for a moment.

"And?"

"The photograph is... very indiscreet," he almost whispered.

"Let me see it," I said simply.

He started like I had fired a shot. "Wh- what?" he stammered.

"You did bring it, didn't you?" I said as plainly as I could. "You wouldn't have been careless enough to leave it anywhere. Which means you must have it with you."

"I don't think you need to see it," Mayfield said firmly. "Janet would be horrified."

"Does she know about it?" I asked.

"No, of course not," he said crossly. "Janet is a very sweet girl. This would devastate her."

"And your wife," I added.

"Of course," Mayfield said as if the thought had just occurred to him. "Of course, her too. But she isn't... Anne isn't in the photograph."

"Just as well," I said. "That sounds like it would be complicated. Show me the photograph or get out of my office."

Roger Mayfield's eyes opened wide and he puffed in protest for a moment. But at last his shoulders sagged in defeat. "Very well," he said, reaching in to his briefcase and pulling an eight-by-ten photograph out of a large manila envelope.

He handed it to me across the desk. For a moment I did not look at it but kept my gaze firmly on Mayfield, as if to reinforce the idea that I had no particular interest in seeing him do his business, which was truer than words could possibly have said.

"Is that the envelope the photo came in?" I asked. He seemed surprised but nodded and handed it towards me. I glanced at both sides of the envelope. One side bore the typewritten address of Mayfield's office at City Hall and the word PERSONAL, underlined in red ink. It told me nothing, but I nodded wisely at it, set it down upon the table and turned my attention toward the photograph.

Very little of Roger Mayfield was in evidence in the photograph. Enough to stand up in court, if it came to that, but he certainly wasn't the star of the show. The picture was taken at a distance, through a window. The bedroom was well-lit and Mayfield, on his back, certainly had no idea he was playing to an audience of more than one. The girl, however, Miss Janet Timms, was a real performer. Her back was arched and a mane of blonde hair was thrown back as if she were in the midst of the most excruciating pleasure. The kind that I found difficult to believe that Roger Mayfield was capable of inspiring, but maybe I was just jealous. Wildly, rabidly jealous.

She was a beauty, that much was for certain. What she was doing with a married, mousey City Planner, beyond the obvious, I couldn't say. I tried to devote no more time to the picture than professional interest would require, and made several entirely fictional notes as I did so.

"Good quality print. Looks professional. Where were you when this was taken?" I said, looking back to Mayfield with as little expression as I could muster.

"Janet's apartment," he said. "Canon Street, near Chapel."

"So it would be, what, second floor? Above some shops?"

He nodded. "That's right."

"So obviously this was taken from across the street with a telephoto lens," I said.

Mayfield seemed oddly surprised. "What makes you say that?" he asked.

"Because I think you might have noticed a peeping Tom on stilts standing in the middle of Canon Street," I said. I glanced back to the print, just for a moment. "Then again, maybe not."

Mayfield flushed and took the photo back from me without comment. He wasn't embarrassed for himself, he was protecting his lady's modesty. This would not be easy.

"Do you usually meet at her apartment?" I asked.

"Yes," he said, "always. Tuesdays."

"You two keep the blinds wide open like that every Tuesday?" I asked.

He seemed a little sheepish. "I couldn't say, Mr. Justice," he said. "I was a little distracted."

I nodded. "Fair enough," I agreed. "What's across the street? More apartments?"

"No," he said, puzzled, "a row of offices. They're always dark. I suppose that's why we never gave them a thought."

I nodded and said nothing. There were two possibilities. Perhaps Janet Timms had an admirer with a very, very good camera who waited untold Tuesdays in the hope that she would one day forget to close the blinds before playtime. With a body like hers, it was hard to argue with that logic, but I didn't buy it. There didn't seem to be any point getting into this with Roger Mayfield just yet. Plenty of time to crush his hopes and dreams later, once he had paid his retainer.

"So someone knows about your affair with Miss Timms," I said as much as possible as if it were the simplest matter in the world. "They have, as yet, made no demands, but it seems likely that will follow. What would you like me to do?"

Mayfield blinked. "I'd like you to take care of it," he said.

"You aren't hiring me to do any murders," I said, filling in the blanks for him, "just to represent your interests in this matter in a lawful manner."

He hesitated at this last part. "In so far as it is possible, yes," he said at last.

"Are you prepared to pay, if necessary?" I asked. "The blackmailer, I mean."

He nodded slowly. "This must be kept quiet, Mr. Justice. Whatever it takes. Find the man who has these photos and deal with him." There was mettle in his stern but purposefully vague assignment that I didn't expect from him.

I nodded. "I get thirty dollars a day," I said, "plus expenses. And I'll need three days in advance."

Chapter Two

The name's Dixon. Trixie Dixon, Girl Detective. That's what it said on my business cards, that's how I answered the telephone and that's what the neatly printed card on the office door read. When you're something of an oddity, you have three choices. You can pretend you really aren't different from the norm at all, in this case I suppose becoming oddly androgynous, like the two or three other lady private eyes of my acquaintance. This was plainly not for me. I'm not vain by nature, but the amount of labor that would be required each and every morning to make Miss Dixon seem mannish would be entirely unreasonable, and for too little return.

Option two, of course, would be to do what Ma and Pa Dixon had always expected – realize that you hadn't a hope of carving out a share of hardboiled human misery for yourself, poor female that you were after all, and meet a nice man, or perhaps go to secretarial school and then meet a nice man. I met lots of nice men. I just didn't keep them around after they stopped being entertaining.

And so I had quickly settled upon option three. The porridge that Goldilocks chose. Since the first thing any prospective client said when they saw me was, "You're a girl!", I took all of the suspense right out of it from the get-go and I never had much cause to regret it.

It was true, I didn't get a lot of the danger and daring-do knocking on my little door. Folks who wanted a thug-for-hire generally went to somebody else. But there was a lot less of that in a private detective's life than the moving pictures would make out, and I did pretty well all things considered.

See, an awful lot of what a real detective does falls in the category of sneaking around, and what better disguise could a private eye have than be a tall blonde with a little too much leg? The first thought through any man's head was not that he ought to behave himself because I just might be a detective there to check up on him. Indeed, it was not in the top ten.

I don't mean to give you the wrong impression. In fact, I wore my girlitude on my sleeve for the benefit of my clientele, who were almost exclusively female. If a lady has the idea that her man has been stepping out behind her back, she doesn't want Johnny Hardboiled and his Gumshoe Orchestra. She doesn't want to tell her story to another man, to feel his leering eyes on her wondering just what it is she does wrong, or doesn't do at all, that sent the wolf of the house out to the henhouse. She wants the straight goods and a shoulder to cry on. It was a solid little niche, even if it did have the cumulative effect of souring a girl on Prince Charming once and for all. The second drawer of my desk was crammed full of hankies and I sent them to the cleaners often enough that the folks at the Chinese laundry must have thought I had an appalling sinus condition or was perhaps allergic to everything.

So to say that I was ready for the waterworks when I saw a shadow fall across my doorway was putting it mildly. I looked up with my most welcoming and sensitive smile from the crossword puzzle I had neatly hidden within a brown file-folder.

What I usually expected to find was a lady standing, red-eyed, hesitating at the threshold, as if taking that final step into my office would spell the end of everything, even if that "everything" was well and truly over already and they knew it full well. It was why I kept the door propped wide open. The little dears would use any excuse to talk themselves out of taking the final plunge into the cold light of truth. Knocking would just be too much for them. And Miss Dixon couldn't have that now could she?

But the sight that met my deep blue eyes on this particular day didn't seem to fit the part. She was put together, composed, maybe even a little amused as she read the card on the door.

"Do you find it necessary to include the 'girl detective' part?" she asked.

"I do," I replied.

"Why is that?" she asked, a sculpted eyebrow raised. "You do not appear otherwise."

"Thanks," I said. "The girls at the beauty parlour will be so pleased."

"I don't mean to offend you," she said, not stepping in. "I was just curious what sort of person you are. The title strikes me as frivolous and I have no need of a frivolous detective."

I stuck my pencil in my up-do in a businesslike fashion. "You must have seen the name somewhere, Ma'am," I said. "The city directory perhaps? Or the ad in the Gazette?"

My guest said nothing, but considered me almost impassively. She also did not step beyond the threshold. This one was a cool cucumber but she was just like all the others. After a moment, she nodded.

"You heard the name and it brought you here," I said. "That's why the 'girl detective' line stays. A sixty-two percent increase in foot traffic since I started using it. Is that serious enough for you?"

She smiled, stepped into the office and closed the door behind her. I made a mental note to keep using the sixty-two percent figure that I had made up on the spot. Whatever works, works.

She sat in my client chair and considered the large closet, or very small office, we were sitting in.

"Not much space," she sniffed.

"I don't go in for dance numbers in the middle of the day," I said without expression.

"You just have an answer for everything, don't you?" she asked.

I said nothing to that, mostly because I knew it would annoy her. She fidgeted with her handbag and I knew that I was right.

"Look," I said by way of a peace offering, "it's pretty clear we both like to be in charge. When you're my client, you are. So let's get to that point as quickly as possible, shall we?"

"Very well, Miss Dixon," she said. "The problem is my husband."

She paused as if I ought to be shocked. I nodded sympathetically, but did not feign surprise. She looked around again. "I half expected tea and doilies," she said.

"Never went in much for doilies," I said. "I'm not above decorating certain things with lace, but furniture isn't generally on the list."

She actually laughed a little at this, just for half a moment. Then she nodded to herself. I could see her figuring it out, finding her feet. After she had dealt with the husband, she was going to try this routine for herself. Confident, brassy, perhaps a secret hellcat. I hoped that she would like it as much as I always have.

"As for tea," I continued, "I've got some around here somewhere. I also have a bottle of scotch in my desk drawer and two fairly clean glasses if that helps us cut to the chase."

She seemed mildly scandalized, but I could tell from the dance in her eyes that the answer was yes. I opened the drawer and produced the goods. Drinking was better than crying, at least for me it was.

"Do you have any ice?" she asked as I poured.

"No," I said without apology. Where would I have been hiding ice?

She took her drink and I took mine. She did not throw it back and hold her glass out for an immediate refill, which disappointed me as I would have been expected to keep pace, but she did take a long sip and swirl the glass as if saying hello to an old friend. I decided that I liked her. I almost always found a reason to come to that conclusion; it made everything that followed that much easier. But with her it wasn't all that hard.

If I had to guess I would say that she was forty, maybe as much as forty-five, but I didn't think so. She had long, raven-colored hair which she wore in a sophisticated up-do. Her clothes were immaculate and fashionable, but not showy. She was the conservative wife of a professional man who never expected to be in this position, but would be damned if she would part with her dignity. I liked her more and took a little of my own drink and waited.

"My husband," she said at last, "is sleeping with another woman."

I nodded.

"This has been going on for quite some time, though I could not say for certain how long."

That didn't seem to need a response, so I kept still.

"My husband is a well-respected professional, and he thinks that is enough," she said. We were entering the monologue now and I knew better than to get in the way. "His reputation means so much to him, but so does his comfort. The comfort that is provided by money. The money that he married into." She paused a little and looked at me as if for effect. I nodded and settled back into my chair. "He loves his place in society, his comfortable home, his pleasant little life with everything just so. But he thinks that he can have all of that, have everything – me, my money, his dignity, and still bounce up and down with his little whore."

She looked at me as if I might be shocked, and when I wasn't, she seemed struck with sudden embarrassment. "I feel as if you are pulling me apart with your eyes," she said as she sipped her scotch again.

"That's part of what I do," I said.

She nodded and said nothing.

"*So you want me to confirm your suspicions about your husband?*" *I asked, reaching for a blank contract in my inbox.*

"*No, Miss Dixon,*" *she said with a snort and threw back the rest of her drink.*

"*Trixie, please,*" *I said, raising the bottle by way of offering a repair.*

She made a motion as if to decline, then changed her mind and held out her glass for a refill of the fine, domestic paint thinner. "*My husband is pathetically predictable. So meticulous in his habits that he could never hope to keep a secret like this for very long. Do you know he sees her on the same night every week? Like a lodge meeting,*" *she snorted again in contempt.* "*What a mad, passionate affair it must be.*"

"*You followed him yourself?*" *I asked, taking a second drink just to be properly sociable.*

"*I did.*" *She tossed her head proudly.* "*I know her address and copied the name from the buzzer.*" *She opened her handbag and passed me a slip of paper.* "*I don't know if it really is her name, but she lives there alone.*"

I sat there being quietly impressed for a moment. Partly because it seemed like the thing to do, partly because it was true. At length I asked the question. "*So what do you need from me?*"

"*I want to be rid of him,*" *she hissed, her anger finally pouring out of her,* "*and I want him left with nothing. I want unquestionable proof of infidelity, the kind that I can make sure people see if he puts up any kind of fight in court. That would destroy him, I know it would.*"

"*You want pictures,*" *I said. It was not a question.*

"*I want him sleeping in a room above a service station,*" *she said with a snarl.* "*I want him cooking on a hot plate, washing his shirt in the sink, thinking every day about the life he threw away. It seems to me that pictures would be the perfect place to start."*

I nodded and slipped two contract forms into the typewriter with a piece of carbon paper.

"I think we can arrange that," I said, all business. "Can we start with your name?"

"Mayfield," she said. "Anne Mayfield."

Chapter Three

I had spent the first day of my service in the employ of Roger Mayfield gathering rosebuds. Which was my way of saying that I was putting together a laundry list of information with which I could answer the nearly inevitable question of exactly what in the hell had I been doing all this time.

It wasn't bad looking, really. Put together with the assistance of Sgt. Ted Holm down at Robbery-Homicide who owed me a favor and my old pal Freddie "the Finger" Hawthorne who owed me more than a few. It was a list of known dirtbags within the city and environs with the requisite photographic skills who had a tendency to lean towards blackmail. The capsule reviews of each man's dossier included his police record, last known location, *modus operandi* and any special proclivities or peccadilloes in which he may specialize. It was all good stuff and looked like it might have taken several days to put together, which was nice because all told it had taken about two and a half hours.

See, in reality, there wasn't a heckuva lot I could do for Roger Mayfield as things stood, try though I might. The ball was in someone else's court. When the blackmail campaign stepped up, I would be there. But it was entirely possible that his mysterious friend would sit quietly for some days and let him stew in his own juices, and if I wished to still be gainfully employed when said scumbag got off the pot, I had better look like I had been doing something.

In reality, of course, the list was useless. Oh, it was accurate, and there was even a chance, if only a chance, that one of the two dozen men it profiled would turn out to be the guilty party. That would make me look pretty slick. But I couldn't very well go knocking on their doors and asking if they knew Roger Mayfield and would they please stop shooting dirty pictures of him and his little blonde vixen of a mistress.

There was really only one more thing that I could do at this point, and only since today happened to be Tuesday. I piled into my old Ford and took spin down Chapel as far as Canon where I stepped out to make a few inquiries. Roger Mayfield had no intention of missing his regular field trip to the scenic sights of Janet Timms, and I couldn't say as I blamed him. I had no trouble spotting her apartment from the street by the window mouldings, and noted with no satisfaction nor surprise that the venetian blinds were down in the bedroom.

Judging from the angle of the photo, or the lack of it really, it seemed pretty clear that our cameraman had been right across the street; the building wasn't hard to spot. I parked the heap on Canon and pulled an old sample case from the trunk. The case was empty, but I had never been much of a brush salesman and didn't figure on getting more than a few words into my pitch. I took a quick look at the lock on the street-level door. If we assumed that our blackmailer did not routinely occupy this building, we must also assume that he got past the lock after-hours. It was an old one; I probably had four or five keys in my pocket that would open it without too much trouble, so that part held. According to the directory in the lobby, the second floor was home to a Notary, a Bookkeeper and an Employment Agency. There was a manual elevator waiting at the ready but I didn't like the look of it and took the stairs.

My career prospects as a brush salesman still appeared to be extremely limited, but I managed to get far enough into my pitch in each of the offices to get a look out the big windows and picked the Notary's office as the most likely candidate. The girl behind the desk was heavyset and a real mouth-breather. I didn't get much more than a peek at her boss, but he struck me as about as sinister as a church mouse. For the moment, I removed them from the list of suspects and went back to the car.

Someone had taken pictures of Janet Timms entertaining my client in a manner most thorough. They had taken them from the Notary's office across the street. That meant this was planned. On the night in question when the Notary's office was broken into, the blinds in Janet Timm's bedroom were wide open and all the goodies on display. Convenient.

There was no earthly reason to believe that our mysterious friend would be watching again tonight. Far from it. Mayfield would be on alert, for whatever that was worth, and blackmailers are by nature craven little cowards. No way they give away their position and then come back to the same duck blind. But it was Tuesday night, I had nothing better to do, and I'd look like a complete moron if I didn't stick around. So I noodled with the radio in the car, wondering if I could tune in the ball game without completely draining the battery. It played hell with my dramatic getaways when I had to get out the jack and turn the crank to get the heap rolling.

I looked up from the dashboard of the heap where I sat and suddenly there she was. Janet Timms, in the flesh. Well, not exactly in the flesh, not as much as I had so recently seen, but she was there right enough, the black Ford parked ahead of me was all that stood between us as she waited facing the traffic on Canon, watching for a slow moment to dart across.

I watched her as she watched the cars. She was a pretty thing, all right. The fading daylight and the full set of clothes made her a little less heart-stopping to be sure, but it was all there. Her dress was brown and seemed simple enough. It looked new and fit her like it was made for her, which I assumed it was. She was wearing a wrap that didn't look quite warm enough for the day, but whether that was bad planning or a general desire to look like a little lost lamb, I couldn't say. Her hat was one of those rounded kinds that hugged the line of the face down past the ears, and her face was narrow enough that the roundness of the hat didn't make her look like a cherub like it did to so many women. It suited her, is all. All of it suited her. It was a carefully prepared effect of casual elegance and possible innocence. The latter I knew to be fraudulent, but I was in no position to hold that against anyone.

The traffic slowed and she made her way across at a trot. I watched her go appreciatively. She didn't look like a tramp or a business girl, but I couldn't accept that the hardware on display would be contented by a scheduled Tuesday tryst. Perhaps she had two or three other Roger Mayfields on the side. That would make a certain amount of sense. If you weren't going to be the kept possession of one very rich man – and there was no reason why Janet Timms couldn't be, I assumed it was because she did not want to be – being the dirty little secret of a handful of reasonably successful men would keep the wolf from the door. And if you turned each one for a big enough payout before the well ran dry and they went back to their wives, well that would be so much the better, wouldn't it?

She disappeared into the doorway that led up to her apartment and I felt a pang of guilt for any number of assumptions I was making, but I was pretty sure that I was right. Girls like Janet Timms did not go for regular guys like Mayfield, however much I and every other regular guy might wish it otherwise. She might not be in on the blackmail, but she'd have her own angle somewhere, and even that was more credit than she deserved.

The real question, and this did bother me a little, was why in blazes Roger Mayfield struck somebody as a swell target for blackmail. Assume the shutterbug was working with Miss Timms. You have the very best bait you could get, and you go after guppies like Mayfield? Quantity over quality? It was safer, I supposed, and maybe the girl enjoyed her work more than I imagined. Some do. At any rate, it wasn't a mystery that Roger Mayfield wanted solved. He had a problem, he wanted it fixed and I was his hired hand. Right now he was unwilling to admit that his bombshell could be involved, so I would let that lie.

But when nothing happened tonight, the options would be to wait and see what developed, or put the scare into Janet Timms and see what shook loose. I decided not to think about that right now. I still had some retainer to burn and could take things as they came.

Chapter Four

There were no other pedestrians on Canon Street when I walked around the corner at Chapel Avenue. That was nice. From a car, nothing that was about to happen would look especially suspicious, especially when performed by a well-dressed young lady such as myself. I came to the lobby door that led to the offices upstairs. I'd taken a peek at the lock when I cased the joint that afternoon, and I was pretty sure that one of the four keys in the palm of my hand would do the trick. As it turned out, it was the second one, and I slipped into the lobby quickly and quietly, locking the door behind me.

I moved at a good pace and didn't try and hide. I was a woman entering a building with a key; no one was going to suspect a thing unless I told them to by acting like a cat burglar. I slipped into the stairwell and moved as quietly as I could through that echo chamber to the second floor.

The first door past the stairwell door was for the Merdson Employment Agency. I was pretty sure the Notary's down the hall would have a better view but I stopped at Merdson's door anyway, having switched one set of keys for another in my bag on the way up the stairs. This time it was the third key that did the trick. It would probably open every door on this floor. I left the door at Merdson's unlocked and tripped merrily down the hallway to Samuel Berker, Notary Public.

As expected, the same key opened Berker's office easily and I slipped into the small space. I had taken a quick glance that afternoon when I had stopped in to ask for directions to somewhere I had no interest in going. I knew that just ahead on the left was the door that led to what I presumed to be Mister Berker's private sanctum. I had not had an opportunity to case the room itself, but I preferred it on spec since it would let me set up without being in full view of the hallway, with the light from the windows behind me creating a shapely but eminently arrestable silhouette.

Berker's office was illuminated by those same streetlights, but by this time my eyes had adjusted to the darkness and I moved quickly. Berker's desk was positioned oddly, facing the window rather than the door. This was nice, as it gave me space to work without shoving furniture around, but it was certainly surprising. I imagined that the daily minutia of a Notary Public was not as exciting as all that. However, this seemed like a great deal of wholesale staring out the window for a man to commit to. The vista wasn't exactly scenic. Canon Street was not renown for its architecture, or for much of anything else for that matter. What was it about the brick wall across the street that little Berker found this compelling?

I set my bag on his desk and opened it. This was not my regular handbag but the big Aunt Gladys model that I used as a de facto camera bag when I had occasion to do so, which was more often than I'd have liked. The camera was a nice piece of equipment, and if you're going to do a lot of lonely hearts club work you've got to have a decent one. I was getting pretty good with it, myself. I wouldn't be winning any prizes, but I'm not at all sure that they had contests for these sort of pictures anyway. Then I thought about it a moment and decided that they probably did and that I didn't want to know about them. There was nothing titillating about what I was about to do, indeed Ma Dixon would have been horrified had I been foolish enough to bring it up.

There was a sudden flash of light from across the street and I ducked instinctively. Then I realized that it was simply the venetian blinds being opened across the way. And all at once I did not wonder why Samuel Berker, Notary Public, stared out the window each and every day.

*The paper my client had handed me said her name was
J. Timms and I had, as yet, taken no pains to confirm that.
She was a knockout. She was dressed to entertain in a light
brown cocktail dress, which hugged her not-
inconsiderable curves in a manner which Samuel Berker
would have given his eye teeth to duplicate.*

*One of the side effects of the life of a detective is that
you start inadvertently turning your own analysis upon
yourself. As I snapped a few test shots of J. Timms
primping and prepping herself and her bedroom for the
evening's work ahead, I knew what I was doing. I was
mentally constructing a list of ways in which my own body
was superior to that of J. Timms, suspected harlot. It was
not, I noted with both professional detachment and gritted-
teeth ire, a very long list, but there were some important
points. I knew that I was doing this because,
subconsciously, I hated being the second fiddle. I knew
that if she saw me, Janet Timms would probably do the
same thing, though she would enjoy the blissful ignorance
of her own motivations that comes with a normal civilian
life. That is, if romancing a husband out from under his
wife each and every Tuesday, regular as Jack Benny,
could be termed normal civilian behaviour. I was starting
to forget.*

*That was another part that bothered me. Tuesdays. I
had seen a picture of my client's husband and he was
nothing to get hot and bothered over. Mrs. Mayfield had
money, which meant that Mr. Mayfield had some to spread
around, but not enough to pay for the apartment across the
way. And I found it hard to believe that J. Timms worked
in a shop or an office like the one I was camped out in.
Maybe I was being unfair, maybe she really did love the
guy and this was the best they could do right now.*

*I watched J. Timms watching herself in the mirror,
straightening her seams. No. I knew a little hellcat when I
saw one. There was no way that a regular Tuesday tryst*

was satisfying that one. So there had to be other marks. Which meant when the hammer came down and the money was gone, Roger Mayfield would get the boot and someone else would get Tuesday nights. I found myself rooting for Samuel Berker. Somebody had to.

A few more clicks of the camera and I had my eye in. All at once the blinds started to bother me. If I were waiting to welcome a lover, I might forget to lower the blinds, but I certainly would not go out of my way to raise them. Miss Dixon is sometimes in a hurry to get to Act II, and while I am not a shy girl by nature, the world is full of Samuel Berkers who do not deserve an eyeful of me however badly they might think they need it.

Of course, it was swell news for me. My client didn't just want the divorce job special – the Mister arriving for his little snack, the silhouettes on the shade, her straightening his tie in the doorway with a pair of dopey post-coital grins on their faces. No, she wanted to humiliate him. She wanted pictures that he would be deeply embarrassed by, though not many men would feel ashamed of proof that they had bedded J. Timms, of that I felt pretty certain. Still, she was the client, and if I could get what she wanted without picking the lock of the apartment across the way and going in camera in one hand, pistol in the other, that would be nice for me. I wasn't above it, but it was undignified.

Something out of the corner of my eye was bothering me all of a sudden, and I took a look at street level to see just what it was. Down the street to my left there was an old black Ford, looked like maybe a forty-one, in pretty poor shape. The car was of no interest, but the alert black shape sitting within was another story. I turned the camera in that direction. I didn't have much of an angle, but he seemed to be looking at the light from the open window even though he couldn't possibly see the goods on display *from where he was. How long had he been there? Was this Roger Mayfield arriving a little early?*

No. The shape was too big and the jaw was too square. I played with the lens a little bit, cursing under my breath that I would need to tune J. Timms in all over again because of ol' Square-Jaw here. I could see him now. Looking casual with such practised ease that it was impossible for me to be sure he was faking it, though I'd have given you odds. Maybe he was waiting for someone. I watched him another five minutes and he hardly moved. What could he be doing? What was he looking at? Suddenly his attention turned to the dashboard of the Ford and I realized in disgust that I had been riveted by a man staring into the middle distance as he listened to the radio. Probably a ball game. Nuts to this.

I turned back to the window. J. Timms was lighting candles on both sides of the bed. She was in a hurry to get to Act II too. If she lit a few more, there just might be enough light. I played with the camera a little, trying to remember the lessons I had coaxed out of a newspaper shutterbug I used to know. At last I felt pretty sure that I would have the low-light settings I needed if the blinds stayed open, and if they didn't, as long as there was a little of the pre-show on display before they were closed, it would probably be enough for Anne Mayfield. Not many housewives actually wanted to see the whole corpus delicti, however much they insisted that they did.

Ten minutes later we were still waiting quietly, J. Timms and I, for the show to begin. She had just taken her first glance down to street level to see if this evening's Prince Charming was about to arrive when I heard a click, quite close to my ear.

I did not move. I am not skittish by nature, but I know the sound of a hammer being cocked when I hear it. This one was a large calibre automatic. Which meant it wasn't a cop. I turned my head as slowly and non-threateningly as I could. It was my friend with the square jaw, and his friend the .45.

"Hi," he said.

Chapter Five

She wasn't what I expected.

Don't get me wrong, a woman will blackmail you, but she'll do it direct. I'd had men march into my office over the years and announce that they were being blackmailed by their hobby women. It usually didn't seem like anything premeditated. More often than not there were promises made, almost always in aid of stripping a lady of her virtue and everything else while they were at it. And when the promises did not come to pass, the lady was angry and wanted to make Mr. Suddenly Happily-Married miserable.

I never took the cases because there was nothing for me to do. Something like that happens to you, there are two choices – bite the bullet or pay the lady. She has no proof, but Mrs. Happily-Married will look Miss Formerly-Enthusiastic Secretary up and down and know damn well what you did. Most of the men who found themselves in this situation were in something of a high dudgeon about it. They reckoned that there should be a third way, and were not pleased to learn this was not a service I provided. If you can ruin a girl yourself, you ought to also be man enough to scare her, if that was what you wanted. And if you couldn't, or wouldn't, don't come crying to the big, bad Jack, because I don't really give a damn.

Most of them took my advice and paid up. They found that I was right; when they paid, that was the end of it. The girl was almost always so disgusted with what she had sunk to that the matter dropped. She hadn't really wanted the money, she had wanted to tell, but she had wanted you to sweat first. To see it coming and be too stubborn to stop it. And when that didn't work, she just wanted to get the hell away from you and get on with her life. It was not a happy ending. But it was an ending.

I did not approve of this kind of transaction, make no mistake. But I was far from qualified on the subject of interpersonal morality, and chose not to cast the first stone. On only one memorable occasion had I become involved in such a case, and that was because the gentleman caller in question clearly wanted the former object of his attention dead. I turned him down politely, found the girl, damn near forced her to hire me, then killed the two men that her former beau eventually found to do the job. That one nearly cost me my license, and would have, except that Police Lt. Sabien, who hated my living guts, hated men who hurt girls even more.

But I digress. I do that.

The point is that a woman will turn on you all right, but she won't often plan it, and she won't often bleed you white. And when she does, it's personal. Blackmailers were an entirely different breed. They were, in the most general of terms, mouth-breathing, pasty-faced scum. Worms that would turn on anyone and everyone, but didn't have the guts to do it to your face. They were dirt. They were also men. Often the kind of men that make you embarrassed to self-apply the term.

All of which is why the blonde in the Notary's office took me by surprise. It wasn't easy to tell in the semi-darkness, but she was maybe twenty-five. Old enough to know better and young enough that she could be playing Janet Timms' role in this little dramatic society if she'd cared to. Maybe that was how they worked it. Two girls in business for themselves. My momentary consideration of this possibility, and the two or three lurid scenarios it immediately caused to burble unbidden into the springtime innocence of my imagination, provided me a suitably menacing pause after my introduction.

"Yes?" the blonde said at last.

"What?" I said, annoyed with her already.

"Did you want something? Because I was kind of in the middle of something here," she said.

"This is a novel line," I said. "Let me guess, you're just here to clean the windows?"

"Don't be stupid," she snapped. "This is a camera, or are you blind?"

"And this is a gun," I said, keeping the .45 nice and level. "And if you were here on any legitimate business, you would have your hands up in front of your face saying 'please don't shoot me' instead of trying to bluff me out."

She thought about this for a second. "Yeah," she said with what was clearly meant to be a distracting smile. "I guess I would."

"So the real question is, who are you, and what are you doing across the street from Janet Timms' apartment with a camera? Put the camera in the bag, by the way. Very, very slowly."

She didn't look happy about it, but she did it. "That's one of the questions, Flat-Top," she said, and how she could tell that with my hat on was anybody's guess. "The other questions are who are you and what are you doing parked down the street in a Ford that looks like Hitler died in it."

"Maybe you're in my office," I said reaching forward and pulling the camera bag toward me, setting it on the desk that sat opposite the window.

"If you're a Notary, I'm Sister Mary Frances," the girl said with a sneer. I put the desk between us and prepared to rifle through her bag with my free hand.

"Nice to meet you, Sister," I said. "Do me a favour and give me a little spin, wouldya?"

The blonde raised an eyebrow. "You're profoundly not my type," she said.

"I'm crushed," I said. "Spin."

"Why?" She didn't even have the common decency to be nervous, just inconvenienced and annoyed.

"If I can't make sure you aren't carrying," I said, "I'll have to knock you out. I don't give a damn, personally, but it'll play hell with that pretty hairdo."

She considered me for a moment and decided that I meant it. She gave a slow, grudging spin. She was wearing a grey skirt that went well below the knee and still managed to show a lot of leg, which was no mean feat. She was fit, probably fast, even in those shoes. She was wearing a white blouse, which might not have been the best choice for a nighttime B&E, but we're all young once. Her jacket was over a chair in the corner and she was nowhere near it, so for the moment I let that go. Blondie was not armed.

"Happy?" she asked as she turned back to face me.

"Overjoyed," I said. "Keep still." I opened the oversized novelty handbag and found a whole lot of nothing other than camera equipment.

"Nice gear," I said.

"Thanks," she said. "I get that a lot. Or were you talking about the camera?"

"You aren't charming your way out of this one," I said.

"Gosh," she said, "and I was so hoping that we'd have a second date. Are you actually looking for ID? You think I'd be stupid enough to bring ID on a Break and Enter?"

"Why not?" I said. "I did. And you were stupid enough to leave a pile of business cards in the bottom of the bag."

Her smile faded at this. I had to squint in the dark and still couldn't quite read them, but it was pretty plain they weren't all the same business card. Or the same business.

"So you're a newspaper reporter," I said.

"That's right." She didn't bat an eyelash.

"And a florist. And you run a secretarial school. And you're a girl detective. That one's adorable by the way." The blonde now looked positively sour. "And you have about sixteen different names. So all we've really established is that you like taking dirty pictures."

"Why?" she asked. "You see anything dirty going on over there?"

I would like to open this portion of the narrative by saying that I know I am a stupid fool for looking. In my defence, I was pretty damn sure that I was in control of the situation. In my further defence, the occupant of the apartment across the way had a figure that could easily have launched a thousand ships and if there was, in fact, something dirty going on, I suppose subconsciously I would not have minded seeing a little bit of it. Shoot me. Which is actually very nearly what happened next.

I was vaguely aware of movement in the corner of my eye. It got my attention, but she wasn't moving her feet and she wasn't within arm's reach of anything that interested me so I didn't sweat it too much. A second later I turned back from the sadly still-clad goddess across the way to the bird in the hand, who now had a nice little .22 in her hand.

I dove to the right as she fired and hit the dirt hard behind the desk. I did this not because I had to, but because my options were restricted to this or splattering Blondie's brains all over the offices of a perfectly good Notary Public. She fired again, taking a fair-sized divot out of the otherwise tidy office furniture. I couldn't imagine what in the hell she was doing. The way was clear, and if the peroxide hadn't rotted her brains away, she'd have been running just in case I was less disinclined towards blowing a lady's head clean off than my track record thus far would have you believe.

That was when I realized that I'd still had my hand on her camera bag when I'd made my dive and it had joined me on the floor. Blondie wanted her camera back and was either prepared to die for it, or hadn't really thought this one through. I hoped it was the latter. The camera was nice, but it wasn't that nice.

Where in the hell she had pulled the pistol from, I couldn't begin to say. That was on me. Full points to her. And yes, in close quarters, a .22 can kill you just as dead as a .45. But she had a clear route to the door and wasn't using it. That was bad math.

I could hear her footsteps on the carpet scrambling for position. She knew she wasn't going to intimidate me, not with a little pea-shooter like that. She was ready to plug me if she had to, to get away clean. I respected that but it also cheesed me off.

Thing is, and yes, there was no way for Blondie to know this, but if I wanted her dead, she'd be dead. She'd have been dead when I walked in the room, she'd have been dead before she pulled the trigger the first time, she'd have been dead about six times in the three and a half seconds since then. I am a killer. I say this with no perverse pride, but simple embarrassment. I do not use the designation merely because I have killed people. Lots of guys my age have killed lots of other guys my age. It was the national pastime of about fifty countries there for a while. But I was a specialist. Uncle Sam taught me to do the job and do it well. Then he pinned a medal on my chest and pushed me off a gangplank, expecting me to be a regular person again. There had been many a sleepless night over things that I had done, then and since. I reckoned there would be more before I finally met a killer better than me, which seemed the only logical end.

It gave a guy a different way of looking at life and death than your average man in the street. It didn't make me better, just different. I worked within the law and I tried to play for the angels as much as I could, but the angels didn't always make it easy. I was a killer. If I wanted you gone, you were gone. That's what set me off when a comedy act like Blondie and her magic disappearing pistol came down the mountain at me. She thought she was playing me to a draw, when all that was keeping her alive was the fact that I was fighting everything I had been taught, and several degrees of basic animal instinct. If she was serious about this, if she didn't wise the hell up and now, I was going to put her in the ground.

Without sticking my nose out, I fired the .45 into the ceiling above her head, and a liberal spray of plaster and dust fell all over the place. A gun like that makes a hell of a racket, and that alone stops most folks in their tracks. Usually you hear a frightened little squeak about a tenth of a second after you fire it, and I was suitably impressed to hear no such noise out of Blondie. But I was pleased to hear what I did. Her footsteps, scrambling out the doorway, at speed.

I could chase her down, of course, but the only thing that might come out of that is a chance to shoot her in the back, and I wasn't big on that either. So my blackmailer got away. Hadn't really expected to find her tonight, much less get a good look at her, much less take her camera from her and get a lead on who she was. And I did it all without getting in the way of my client's Happy Hour, which I assumed he was now having since when I turned back to Janet Timms' apartment, the blinds were drawn. He wouldn't make that mistake again. We were going to call this one a decent day's work for the forces of law and order, and if the gunshots didn't bring the cops down on my head before I could get back to the car and get out of Dodge, I thought I might celebrate with a beer or six and try not to think about what a lucky bastard Roger Mayfield was.

Good times.

Chapter Six

I hit the hallway at full tilt and pushed it into another gear I didn't know I had for the twenty feet or so of straightaway ahead. If the idiot with the square-jaw wanted to think that I was running like a frightened bunny before the awesome might of his shots at nothing in particular, that was just fine. I had to make time if this was going to work. Dingus would need to get back on his feet and get out from behind the desk before he could get after me at all, and that's if he charged right out like a bull moose. My bet was that he hung back at least five seconds to make sure I wasn't waiting just beyond the door of Sam Berker's little office, ready to put a hole in his head.

Never get in a firefight if you don't absolutely have to, or at least really, really want to. That was my motto. It would sound better once I had it translated into Latin. The corollary to that rule, of course, was to never stay in a firefight longer than was absolutely necessary. Tall, Dark and Stupid didn't strike me as all that good at whatever it was he did for a living, but he did manage to get the drop on yours truly so I gave him some otherwise unearned credit. Let us assume that my long and shapely neck was at a certain amount of risk shooting it out at close quarters.

Yes, I had broken a couple of laws tonight, but the most serious had been the moment that I fired the .22. I had no regrets, apart from the fact that the little pop-gun pulled high and to the left, wrecking the molding on Samuel Berker's door frame rather than putting one in Pork-Chop's shoulder and sitting him down for questioning...

No. It's a poor workman who blames her tools. The gun didn't pull, I missed. I needed to work on targeting on quick draws with my little hidden piece, but for three or four reasons, that was a bit awkward. Miss Dixon already garnered too much attention at the shooting range.

So now I had two problems. Well, okay, there were more, there were two that I was prepared to worry about this very second. I had some hat-rack on my tail, and he had my camera bag. Fortunately, I was prepared for just such an emergency.

He would hit the hallway any second. The elevator was right there, and the stairwell beside it. He had to assume that was where I had gone, and if he wanted to meddle with me badly enough to have done what he did, he would follow rather than admit to whoever put him up to this that I got away. I was fast, but he had a shot at me on those stairs. Except I wasn't going to be anywhere near them.

I hit the door of the Merdson Employment Agency hard and rolled backwards as I pushed my body past the barrier. The way behind was still clear. I pushed the door closed and froze, not moving a muscle that might betray me. This is why I had unlocked the door as I passed it on the way in. Circumstances dictated that I had no choice but to put myself into a box with one way out, but at least I could construct myself a bolt-hole. This was so close to where I started no one would ever think of checking the door. Square-Jaw would blunder past at full speed making for the stairwell. He'd be halfway down before he was sure that he couldn't hear me just ahead of him and would take the rest of the stairs and stick his fool head out the door to check the street before he would even begin to accept the truth.

By the time it occurred to him that I might have never left the second floor, if indeed such a notion did penetrate his meaty brow at all, I would have stepped lightly back into Chez Berker, collected my goodies and exited by the unmarked service stairs at the far end of the hallway, down what looked at first to be a dead-end. Perfect.

Sixty seconds later, it was starting to feel less perfect. There was no sound from the hallway. Nothing. I found myself wondering if he could have been hit after all. I was already in a certain amount of trouble, but if I left the big idiot to die, that would be worse.

I replayed both shots I had fired in my mind. I could see the impact of the first bullet, wide and to the left. The second shot had been nowhere near the lummox. I had bounced it off Samuel Berker's desk and wrecked the wall behind his chair. It wasn't a shot at anything, it was to keep him down while I figured out what to do. No way it hit him, no way.

Another two minutes went by. He was just bothering me now. He couldn't have figured out where I was, and if he had, why wouldn't he have burst in the door? If he were really all that scared of being shot he wouldn't have come up here in the first place, he'd have called the law when he saw me in the window.

I could feel my brow knit in irritation. And just how exactly had he seen me up here? I wasn't invisible, but you'd have had to be looking, and more to the point, you'd have had to be looking with the expectation of seeing something. And you'd have had to care, for some reason. None of it made a whole lot of sense.

Could he have been J. Timms' actual gentleman friend? Making sure that all was well, if from afar? No. That seemed a stretch. First of all, I couldn't accept that a quality bit of merchandise like J. Timms would give herself freely to ol' Square-Jaw. Secondly, even if she did, having him hang around at street level while she punched the clock with my client's husband seemed cold. So maybe it was a professional arrangement?

Except Roger Mayfield wasn't rich. Not really rich, not Sugar Daddy rich. No doubt he was helping to pay for the apartment across the way, but he couldn't be picking up the entire tab. And even if she had six others, which would never give her a night off, it seemed unlikely that she could also be supporting a staff. Or a pimp. There was nothing in particular to suggest that Mayfield was paying J. Timms, and however much my client may have enjoyed her therapeutic use of the word "whore", it was almost certainly applied in the pejorative sense, rather than a strictly literal one.

All of this was very interesting. Where in the hell was the big idiot with the .45?

It had now been at least five minutes. What if he were standing in the hallway, waiting for me? Worse, what if the shots fired brought a prowl car down here? And what if they actually did their jobs and got out of the car and checked the street level door? Seemed like a stretch, but Miss Dixon could find herself at the tender mercies of John Law, and they never did like me all that much. Well, certain individual representatives of the force had, upon occasion, liked me a great deal in a purely unofficial capacity, but that was at least somewhat beside the point. As an organization, they mostly did not, let us leave it at that.

This was really starting to bother me. I was actually being quite clever, and I hated it when people failed to appreciate that properly by doing exactly what I expected them to. Even if the big ape was silent as a kitten on his feet, I'd have heard the elevator or the door to the stairwell opening. Which meant he had to be there still. Didn't it?

I opened the door to the Merdson Employment Agency nice and slow. Nothing. I eyed the stairwell. It seemed like the better part of valor, but that camera was too much of my bread and butter, to say nothing of the fact that one of the business cards in the bag belonged to the actual Trixie Dixon, and we couldn't have that.

I stepped silently down the hall back toward Samuel Berker's door, unable to believe I was doing this. Technically it was not my fault if the gunsel had a heart attack or something. I'd given a man one before and not been charged with anything. The circumstances were, admittedly, dramatically different.

I stepped back into Berker's office. I wished I had my Beretta. It had some weight, felt bona fide in my hand. This is not what the .22 was really for. I heard a floorboard creak under my foot and closed the rest of the distance between the inner office and myself as fast as I could.

Nothing.

The office was empty. No big dumb ape. No camera bag. He had known about the service stairs too. He may not have known where I was, but he knew I'd try something to get that camera back and get away clean, and he'd stepped past the whole issue while I was lying in wait like an idiot. I resolved to shoot him next time we met, on general principles.

Except there might not be a next time since I had no idea what he was doing here in the first place. If I stuck close to J. Timms he might turn up sooner or later, though what I was supposed to do about J. Timms and R. Mayfield without a camera was not immediately clear to me.

I glanced across the street. The blinds were now drawn and the flicker of the candlelight showed through, though no motion could be seen. Perhaps it was over already. Poor girl, she wasn't having any more fun than me.

I was about to leave when I spotted something on Samuel Berker's desk that did not belong. A small rectangle of white in the semi-darkness. It was a business card, and it wasn't one of mine.

I picked it up. It had been lying face-down with a handwritten message on the back. The front of the card read:

Jack Justice Investigations.

The note on the back said, "This one is real."

Chapter Seven

"I dunno, Jack," Ted Holm said with a shake of his head, "the whole thing sounds pretty stupid to me."

Holm was a city cop, a Sergeant at Robbery-Homicide in fact, but he was all right. We knew each other from the war and that was enough for him and it was enough for me. Circumstances dictated that we were on different sides often enough, but it wasn't personal with Ted the way it was with some of the others.

See, there are few things more annoying to a cop than the thought of a detective who can turn down a case and who isn't required to fill out thirty-one flavors of paperwork every time he scratches his behind. The whole idea of a detective-for-hire sets their teeth on edge as though their pensions were somehow at stake. I did very little to endear myself to the local constabulary, it was true. Most of the department would have given me the runaround on spec, before they even really knew what I wanted. Not so Sgt. Holm. We sat at his desk in a corner of the squad room with two genuinely lousy cups of coffee.

"I can't believe they make you drink this," I said, staring at the thick sludge in the bottom of my cup.

"Technically, they don't," Holm said. "And it isn't any worse than it always is, but you drank it anyway."

"You know what the first problem with this coffee is?" I started.

"Jack, I don't want to talk about the stupid coffee," he said.

I blinked at him. I understood all of those words, but strung together in that order they made no sense.

"Sorry," Ted said, aware of having given offense. He always was too decent a guy to be a cop, but he wasn't good for much else and sometimes you did get to shoot people, which he didn't enjoy but was quite good at. "It's just I was wondering if we could cut to the chase a little bit, on account of Lieutenant Sabien is on duty just now."

"That man is crazy about me," I said. "It's getting a little embarrassing."

Ted didn't even respond to that directly but just cleared his throat, as if invoking Sabien might bring down his wrath. I wasn't quite as concerned. I didn't work for Sabien, and hadn't really committed more than a couple of crimes tonight, neither of which he knew about.

Ted broke up my reverie. "The chase?" he asked.

"The meat of the matter, my dear Inspector Lestrade," I began, "is that I expect to see Legs again, having rather pointedly stuck my tongue out at her at the end there. And I would like to know just exactly who she is."

"You sure she went back and found your card?" Ted asked. Of course I was not.

"Of course I am," I said.

"Sounds like you put the scare into her pretty good," he said.

"No," I said. "This one doesn't scare. She just knows the odds."

"I thought you said she was a blackmailer," Ted frowned.

"She is," I agreed.

"Blackmailers are born scared," he said, taking another pull on the grey liquid in his cup.

"Yeah," I deadpanned, "it's a mystery. Will you just stop being such a cop for a minute and help me?"

Holm seemed mildly surprised by this. "And just what exactly was it that motivated you to come down here and confess to at least two crimes if it was not the fact that I am a cop?"

"If I wanted confession, I'd go to a priest," I said.

"Are you even Catholic?" Ted frowned. He was, and didn't think other people should get to joke about it.

"No, I'm a Hindu."

"Tell that to the last steak you ate," he snorted.

"I never said I was a good Hindu," I punctuated the line with my coffee cup, as was my wont, which almost led to my accidental ingestion of still more cop-shop coffee.

"Seriously, Justice," Holm said, "why bring this to me?"

"Because the lady in question was a leggy blonde," I said gravely, "and you are an enthusiast on the subject, not unlike myself and coffee. Which says something very sad about at least one of us."

"Now you're talkin'," Ted grinned. "How long was the hair again?"

"Up," I shrugged.

"Tight little caboose, you say?" Sgt. Holm had his thinking cap on.

"Like a snare drum," I said. "I'm not really expecting you to pull a name from the clear blue sky, you know."

"Oh," he said, disappointed.

"She may not have a record, but she learned the rough talk somewhere and she's up to her neck in this Mayfield thing. I thought maybe these names would ring some bells."

I handed him the mitfull of business cards Blondie had left in her bag. He shuffled through them and snorted.

"What is it?" I asked.

"This one, the florist," he said. "The address on the card is Two Twenty-Six Sycamore."

"So?"

"So that's the address of the Four Roses Bar & Grill. Roses, florist. It's cute."

"I don't really do cute," I frowned.

"You should," he said. "It's fun. A lot of these have a little joke in there somewhere. Look at this one. Decent little press pass for the *Gazette*."

"Yeah?"

"So that isn't the right address. That's the place across the street where all the reporters get loaded after deadline. What is it, Greeny's?"

"Greevey's," I said. "So she has a sense of humor and likes a drink. Doesn't tell me much."

"Tells me plenty," Ted grinned again. "We have got to find this girl."

"How is Eileen gonna feel about that?" I asked.

Ted scowled. "You leave Eileen out of this," he said with a look like I'd stepped on his grave.

"Maybe I should take Blondie's camera and go into business for myself," I said.

"First lesson," he scowled, "never blackmail the poor." Suddenly his face lit up as he shuffled through the deck in his hand. "Well, I'll be damned," he said.

"What is it?" I asked. "More comedy card capers?"

"Yeah," he smiled. "Mystery solved, Ace." He held aloft the one that read, *"Trixie Dixon, Girl Detective"*.

"Yeah, I saw that," I scowled. "Hilarious."

"And accurate," he said. "She's real. And she's an eyeful."

I stared at him and said nothing.

"I'm not lyin', Jackie," he said. "Tall leggy blonde, full of sass. Licensed private detective."

"God help us all," I said with a shake of my head.

"It's the wave of the future, Jack," he grinned.

"They'll be Homicide cops next," I said.

"Don't be stupid," he frowned.

"So you know her?" I asked.

"Not as well as I'd like," he said clicking his teeth.

"Eileen would be thrilled," I said. "You've onlyadmired from afar?"

"Sure," he said, "but only 'cause I haven't had a chance to get anear."

"That's cute," I said.

"Thanks," he said. "I've been saving that one. Don't know much about her. Set up shop almost a year ago. Does a pretty good trade with the ladies. Surprised to see her working a blackmail racket." He shook his head. "Don't sit quite right."

"Tell that to Roger Mayfield," I said.

"You do take a few dirty pictures now and again yourself, you know," Holm said, going back for still more of his coffee. "It is kind of part and parcel of the peeper trade."

I frowned. It was probably true, but he still shouldn't say it. "So why would she send my client a snapshot of himself playing the role of Seabiscuit in a match race on Cannon Street?"

Holm shrugged. "Maybe she's working for the blackmailer?"

"You know a lot of blackmailers who hire private eyes to do their dirty work for them?" I asked.

Holm shrugged again. He was getting good at that. If he did less thinking he'd make Lieutenant. "Not a bad cover," he said, "but it cuts into the profit margin, and this isn't exactly a Rockefeller getting squeezed, is it?"

"It is not," I said. "So let's keep it uncomplicated, if we can."

"Well," he said, "she does have a record."

I blinked at him two or three times.

"A record," he said again, as if this explained everything.

"For what?" I asked.

The shrug appeared again. "No idea. It's a juvie. And juvies are sealed."

"So unseal it," I said.

"Is that a court order?" he asked with a raised eyebrow.

"It is not," I admitted.

"Then no can do," he said. "Besides, I don't have it handy or anything."

"How do you know this, anyway?" I asked.

He smiled. "When a policeman admires a lady from afar," he said without embarrassment, "a background check is a standard investigative tool. In case it makes it easier to strike up a conversation later."

"Charming," I said. "I'm telling Eileen on you."

"No you won't," he said. "You're more scared of her than I am. And if you do, I'll arrest you on the B&E and unlawful discharge of a firearm."

"Get started on the paperwork," I said, "and add something about blackmail. It'll give you more time for conversation when I bring you 'Trixie Dixon, Girl Detective'."

"And here it isn't even my birthday," he beamed.

A voice thundered from the other side of the room, far above all of the normal din. "What in my Aunt Fanny's gout is *he* doing in my squad room!?"

I turned and saw the majestic form of Lieutenant Victor Sabien stomping toward me at speed. He was a big guy, a real cop not a politician, who had risen from thick-necked bull to head of Robbery-Homicide by being good at what he does, which is not the same as being a decent human being. Sabien didn't care for me. At all. I smiled at Ted, who had turned pale at the sight.

"Gotta go, Teeder," I grinned. "Thanks for the coffee."

Chapter Eight

It was six o'clock in the morning, and I was ready to hand Square-Jaw his big, ugly hat.

I'm not entirely sure what he expected when he left me his business card, but I had the Beretta in my bag now and was through playing games. His exit from the office of Samuel Berker was pretty slick, I was willing to give him that on points, but then he had to go and lose the lightning round by leaving me his address like a stupid kid showing off.

What kind of name was "Jack Justice" anyway? How seriously was I supposed to take this guy? I get that it could be tough for a fella to get a start as a Private Eye with a name like Emil Meeker or something, but do you really have to go a hundred and eighty degrees in the opposite direction with the pseudonym? I wondered about the list of names he had rejected. Hunky McMann? Lance Strongchin?

I was keeping a low profile in the window of a coffee shop on the other side of Lake Street. The coffee was uniquely terrible and seemed to have been boiling for a couple of days until it was all roughly the texture of that skin you sometimes find on a bowl of soup. It was bad all right, but it was still too quiet on the streets to be waiting openly.

I had been up to the palatial offices of Jack Justice Investigations already, just on the off chance that the genius dropped my camera bag off before retiring for the night. The elevator had a sign posted on it that read, "Out of Order", which did not look all that new. Some helpful wag had thoughtfully added the note "AGAIN" in pencil, so it looked like the office was essentially in a walk-up.

The lock had been tougher than I expected, but still didn't present that much of a challenge. Inside there were two desks, two chairs, two of everything that might suggest there were two detectives on the job. The moniker on the door showed no sign of a partner, unless there were two Emil Meekers, each taking turns at being Jack Justice. Seemed unlikely, but if this bozo was doing well enough to afford a secretary, I was prepared to quit the business on principles.

But it was not the case. One desk was mostly empty, and the stuff piled on top of it seemed to have been placed there from the other side, as if it had become the catch-all spot for anything that the great detective didn't really want to put away just now.

The other desk was neater, but only just. I couldn't find any contracts more recent than 1947, but in what I assumed to be the inbox there was a carbon copy pulled from a receipt book made out to Roger Mayfield. The paper was otherwise unrevealing, it just said, "Retainer". People usually tore up any paperwork linking them to a private detective as soon as they were out of your office but that was no excuse for not keeping contracts for yourself. There were filing cabinets full of case files, however one had not been started for Roger Mayfield yet, if indeed it ever would. Swell.

Still, that seemed to be the solution to the great mystery of Jack Justice's timely arrival at Sam Berker's door. He was working for my client's husband, but as what? And why? Was he a bodyguard? If so, why had he been travelling without Mayfield? And why had he left while Mayfield was presumably still playing cat and mouse with J. Timms, dragon lady?

There had been no answers, and I had regretted getting up quite this early in the morning. Square-Jaw kept a coffee pot in the corner that looked like a veteran of the Crimean War, and I toyed with the idea of putting it on and making camp at the empty desk, but the idea was to try and avoid a shootout if at all possible, so I made for the place across the street and waited.

Half an hour later, I was in a foul mood, and it wasn't just because the unshaven lump of a man who seemed to own the place kept refilling my cup. It was because I knew that I had missed an elementary piece of deduction, and I hated it when I did that. Why would a man like Jack Justice, who did not strike me as unduly domestic, keep a station in his office to make his own coffee when he had a coffee shop across the street? Answer: because the coffee across the street would eat the lining out of your stomach in twenty minutes.

I decided to take my chances out on the street. I eyed the neighborhood. Not exactly glamorous, but I didn't know of a lot of detectives with what you might call a great location. It wasn't an impulse buy sort of business, and there didn't seem to be much point in paying for frontage. People found you when they needed you, and when they walked in your door, they didn't really want anybody they might know to see them do it. Later on they'd refer you to everybody they knew. It was fun to be the one who knew a reliable detective, like an honest plumber. But when their troubles were still legion, that was not the time to be public.

The traffic was starting to get heavier now. Even here there was a morning rush. People and cars everywhere, I had no worries about standing out, except for reasons that I usually did and there wasn't a whole lot I could do about that.

There was a construction crew on the sidewalk to the east of Justice's building and they looked like they had been there for a few days at least. There was no getting through that way, which meant he'd have to come from the west, or from the other side of the street which was territory currently held by yours truly. So in any case, I was certain to see him.

I expected him to be early. That's what I would do, and it seemed like what any sensible professional would do

*when there was an opponent who knew who you were and
where to find you. Avoid them, be early, be settled in your
space with a hidden pistol under the table when they
arrived.*

Not Jack Justice. Idiot.

*It was now quarter to nine, and I was getting fed up. I
should have surprised him in his office. I should have
found out where he lived and run him over in my car. I felt
like a fool wandering the street, and felt like everyone I
saw knew that I had been there for hours, when in reality,
it couldn't have been more than a few shopkeepers that
noticed. I'm not sure what bothered me more, the fact that
some of them must surely think I was a prostitute by now
in spite of my conservative, professional attire, or the fact
that they must also think I was a depressingly stupid
prostitute for hawking my tawdry wares in a terrible
location and getting no offers to boot. If I did get an offer,
I was going to shoot someone, that much was clear to me.*

*By ten-fifteen I was leaning up against a lamppost like
a juvenile delinquent, wishing that I smoked cigarettes so I
would have something to do. My plan had started out as a
reasonable discussion with my opposite number, and
shifted over time to sticking him up for my camera bag
when he walked up the front steps of his office building. An
hour ago I had fully intended to shoot him in the chest as
soon as I saw him, regardless of how many people could
ID me to the cops. A guy like this must have a hundred
people who want him dead. But now I was just bored out
of my tree.*

*At ten thirty-five, the morning traffic had slowed to a
crawl and everyone who was going somewhere was now
more or less there. There would be a hubbub of activity in
the noon hour, but for now, the neighborhood was nicely
tucked in and no Jack Justice. My feet were killing me. I
peeled my tired eyeballs off the scenic vistas of Lake
Street. My gaze rolled up to the windows above and settled*

on a familiar shape in an unexpected place. There, in what had to be the large window behind the occupied desk, was Jack Justice, taking photographs of me with my own camera.

He saw me see him, of course, that had been the point. God only knows how long he had been standing there. I felt my eyeballs shake in fury as I pushed myself away from the wall, glaring daggers at the window above. He moved the camera away from his face and gave me a small wave, a lampoon of a friendly neighbor across a fence. I pointed at him, and I'm not really sure what I was trying to say with that, beyond the fact that my heart was full of hate and it seemed like the thing to do.

He reached for something that was hidden by the window frame and held aloft a coffee cup, from which he drank, having first toasted me. It seemed like an invitation, and whether it was or not, that's what I was going to take it as. I took the Beretta from my bag and held it by my side, all business. There was, I confess, nothing but murder in my heart. The city with which I was in some small way charged to protect would be a better, safer and less stupid place when Jack Justice was dead.

I took three steps out into the now-quiet stretch of Lake Street. I was, at that moment, both brandishing a firearm and jaywalking, though I did not expect quite the immediate response from the city's finest that I got.

In that instant, there was a convergence of prowl cars, at least four, with sirens muted but lights flashing. There could have been more, I couldn't say for sure, but there was also at least one unmarked car with them, all parked quite suddenly, higgledy-piggledy every which way, the only common theme being that they all stood between me and the steps of Jack Justice's building.

The doors flew open, and one attentive blue-coat noticed the hardware by my side and drew his own weapon, hollering for me to stop where I was. Most of his

*brother officers were rushing up the stairs into Justice's
building and two were running into the alley where I
presumed the fire escape he must have climbed to avoid
me could be found. They had clearly made this trip before
and knew the tricks.*

*I was keeping quite still, being far too attractive to be
used for target practice, and my prom date with the police
special seemed a little rattled by the fact that I had not yet
dropped the Beretta, which he had not actually told me to
do. The doors of the unmarked car flew open and a couple
of hundred pounds of broken-down ex-beat cop lumbered
out gracefully. I knew this one. His name was Sabien, and
we had shared tea and cookies once or twice before.*

*"Drop it before he shoots you, princess," Sabien
growled at me. "He's a timid little cupcake, aren't you,
Foley?"*

*The patrolman flushed and set his jaw angrily. I did not
bother arguing either, but dropped the Beretta as gently as
I could. "I have a permit for that," I said.*

*There was a ruckus from the building across the way,
suggesting that the strong-arming of Jack Justice might
not be going quite as smoothly as planned.*

*"What's this all about, Sabien?" I called. He ignored
me and turned his attention momentarily to Foley.*

*"Cuff her and throw her in the back, if you can manage
it," he snarled, "and radio base and have them call off the
unit at Dixon's office."*

*My head was spinning. I hadn't had quite enough sleep
to be sure, but I was pretty sure I hadn't shot anybody yet.
Four officers came out the front door carrying my
intended victim by a different limb each. I got the
impression that everyone involved had done this before.
Jack was singing "Onward Christian Soldiers", loudly
and with no apparent knowledge of what most of the words
were.*

I felt the cold steel of the handcuffs click around my wrists, and the strong grip of Officer Foley on my arm leading me towards one of the prowl cars.

All right. Now I was mad.

Chapter Nine

I was back at Robbery-Homicide, and had been for over an hour. They had me in room number six which was one of the small ones, just me and two suits I didn't know particularly well. I half-expected a good going-over, but they were all business. Kept on me about every little detail about my date with Blondie in the Notary's office, and I knew that Ted Holm had given me up to Sabien. I didn't begrudge him that, a fella's got to live after all, and I had expected it. But I had also expected Sabien to cuss Ted out and that to be the end of it. They were taking this all way too seriously.

The detectives applying the questions were named Long and Bradley. I felt like there might be a joke in there somewhere, but it never quite came to me. They seemed half-disinterested in this activity as though they regarded it as a waste of time, but cops do that sometimes in the hopes you'll let your guard down. If they're talking to you at all, it was best to assume that they were dead serious. After half an hour they switched gears again and I realized that I had been right, they were playing me. Now they were playing angry, but doing it badly. I had been through the story just as I told it to Ted, but leaving out the name of my client. That was none of their business, and giving it up was bad business for me. There was a good chance that they already knew it, but from the way they kept harping on it, I got the feeling that Holm might have left it out too. The cops and I had played this little game a few times before. I was of the opinion that my clients were entitled to confidentiality, like a lawyer. The cops thought that was very cute, but since there was no such law forcing them to respect that, they would like me to spill, and do it before they got angry. It never amounted to very much, but it was usually enough to get me before a review board.

This had me going through a mental checklist as I ran through the events of the previous night for the seventh time. I was trying to think if I had done anything lately that would make it seem worth their while to have my license pulled. Again, I came up zeroes. I had actually been pretty good lately. That is, assuming that they didn't know about the Brusci case, and since I was not actually in a cell right now, I was going to assume that they did not. So what in blazes was this tap-dance about? If there were two cops in with Blondie too, plus the swarm they brought to collect me, this was all turning into quite a little operation. And if it was in aid of anything more than Sabien being a general pain in the nether regions, I couldn't imagine what it could be.

At last the door opened and a uniform named Green stuck his head in. He looked serious. My friends in room number six looked serious. Everybody was serious except me.

"Anything?" Green asked.

"Nothing new," Long answered.

Green nodded. "He's ready," he said.

Oh good. Barring the unscheduled arrival of an angry, Old Testament God, there was only one "He" in Midtown that was going to inspire that kind of gravity down at Robbery-Homicide. I was, at last, being brought to an audience with the big man.

Sabien had selected room number three for this. One of the larger rooms, and with a full wall of mirrors that I had to assume served to conceal an unknown number of spectators. There couldn't actually be any – who on Earth would they sell tickets to this circus to? But it was a big stage, and Sabien liked a big stage.

Bradley opened the door and I stepped in as if to a round of applause. It was always best to assume the crowd was on your side, if it existed. Tragically, the object of my affection failed to be annoyed by my manner. Sabien had not yet arrived. Always the showman.

I sat down and handed Bradley his handcuffs, which I had removed on the way over from room six.

"Sorry," I smiled, "they were itching."

Bradley did not smile. Cops hate nothing quite so much as a guy that can get out of handcuffs. I stretched my arms casually, as if to rub it in. Bradley looked around, and I could tell that he was wondering if anyone was behind those mirrors too. If there was, and he tried to put the cuffs back on me before Sabien arrived, he would only look like an idiot and he knew it. He ran his fingers through his Brylcreemed hair in frustration and turned on his heel, closing the door behind him. I was alone. I waggled my fingers in a fey wave toward the mirrors. If there was nobody there, I looked silly and no one knew it. If there was an audience, I was annoying them, and that was what was important.

The door opened and two officers brought Blondie in and sat her down beside me. One of them left the room, the other stayed behind, possibly to make sure we didn't pass notes or chew gum.

"Princess," I said by way of acknowledgement.

"Don't talk to me," she deadpanned. "Don't talk to me, don't look at me, don't even think about talking or looking."

"Can I think about knocking your teeth in?" I smiled.

"Dream big, Peaches," she said.

She did a little double-take and I could tell that she noticed my lack of handcuffs. I smiled and rubbed my wrists. "Want me to take yours off too?" I asked.

She seemed to think about this for half a second. "No," she said.

"Good," I smiled as the door opened and Sabien walked in.

Sabien was a big guy, and for all the years since he'd left his Blues behind, wearing a suit still didn't seem to agree with him. He wasn't in bad shape for a guy who spent a lot of time behind a desk, but he sweated a lot, mostly around the back of his neck. He mopped his neck with a handkerchief, but the heat he was generating back there had the effect of keeping his aftershave at full strength all day. He always smelled a little like your dad's medicine cabinet.

Sabien sat down. He glared at the girl. He glared at me. He glared at my wrists. My wrists and I sat there and took it.

"Who cuffed you?" he asked, as quietly and calmly as he had ever asked anything.

"Originally?" I asked. "No clue. It was a group effort. And lay off them, you wouldn't have done any better."

Something like a crooked smile played around his face and it made me freeze a little around the boots in spite of myself. One of the advantages of being a sour, angry man is that a little smile becomes the most disarming device you could hope to have. Sabien played it well.

"I think I could keep a pair on you," he purred like a tiger with a toothache. "That little trick don't work so good when you've got two broken elbows."

I nodded. There was no point pressing him for a demonstration. "I concede the point," I said. "Can we go now?" The blonde seemed to start a little at this, as if she objected to my referring to us as "we".

Sabien just looked at me and opened a case file. It was surprisingly thick, which suggested that he had chosen a pretty poor prop.

"Oh for Pete's sake, Sabien, enough with the little theatre society. I'm not buying it," I said.

"Will you just shut up so we can find out what this is about?" It was her. She was not helping.

"Grown-ups are talking right now, baby," I said.

"You call me baby again," she snapped, "and I will pull your liver out with my teeth."

"You keep coming on to me," I said, "but I'm just not interested. It's a little sad."

"You two comedians do realize that I'm sitting right here?" Sabien seemed annoyed, but also a little curious.

"One second, Sabien," she began as if there was to be a great deal more.

"No, Dixon!" Sabien barked. "This is my party and I say you sit down and shut up."

I declined to mention that the girl detective was, in fact, already sitting. In fact we all agreed to let that go. Sabien looked back to his case file.

"Enough with the gag file, Sabien," I said. "What is this really all about?"

"Gag file?" Sabien got quiet. That was a bad thing. When Sabien had nothing, he got loud. But he was quiet. Like he was holding a straight or better. "You think I'm here to kid you?"

I had, of course. But now I wasn't so sure. Still, may as well see the bit through. "Get off it, Lieutenant. What have you got? Petunia and I took a couple pot shots in one another's general direction, but I missed on purpose and she couldn't hit the broad side of a barn."

"Drop dead, ape," she snapped.

"And in any case, none of that means a thing unless we start preferring charges against each other," I said, which shut the girl up. At last. "So what have you got? A damage complaint from the Notary? Fifty cents worth of plaster and a little paint. You've got her on a petty B&E if you like. Me, I didn't B, I just E'd."

Dixon glared daggers at me. Sabien had a look like he was waiting to hit me with an anvil the moment I shut up, so I didn't.

"So you've had a good laugh and you've made your point and while I cannot speak for the girl detective, I suspect that we have both learned our lesson," I said. "Can I go now?"

Sabien said nothing, but opened a box that was beside him on the table. From it he produced my .45, the Beretta I had seen in Dixon's hand out on the street, and the little .22 she had used the night before. Sabien looked at us as if he had produced a rabbit from his hat.

"I gotta ask," I said, "where did she have the .22?"

"Go to hell," Dixon snapped at me.

"Little holster, strapped to her thigh," Sabien said with a raise of his eyebrow.

I laughed out loud. The girl's ears turned bright red, but her face looked even more sour.

"A mousetrap hidden on the way to the cookies, is that it?" I asked.

She looked like she was going to leap to her feet and make good her threat on what was left of my liver. Sabien put a stop to that with an open-handed slap on the tabletop that echoed around the room like a gunshot. He had done that more than once, and it showed.

"Two officially licensed, highly trained private-type detectives," he began quietly, "each working for persons unknown, each watching the apartment of one Janet Timms. Each, for whatever it is worth, armed to the teeth. And with a camera thrown into the mix for good measure."

Sabien was building up to something. He reached into the folder and flipped an eight by ten photograph our way. It spun and stopped between Dixon and I, showing the inside of Janet Timms' apartment from an angle I had not seen before. And there was Timms, still mostly beautiful, all but for the hole in her head.

"So you two geniuses want to explain how, with the both of you watching, Janet Timms went and got herself dead?"

Chapter Ten

The cop opened the door to the consulting room and directed me in with a little push that was meant to seem tough. "You've got ten minutes," he said.

The long brunette seated at the table didn't even look up from her paperwork. "We've got however long I say we've got, little man," she said frostily, "and don't you forget it."

The cop said nothing, but made the tactical error of not running away. Molly Cameron looked up at him and smiled condescendingly, as the lady of the manor might toward the deformed, idiot servant boy. "We'll let you know if we need anything," she said.

The cop closed the door, muttering impotently to himself as he did so. I sat down at the table across from my attorney who put her papers away in an unhurried fashion. Molly Cameron did everything in an unhurried fashion. She moved like a panther that got paid by the hour. I liked her anyway.

"Molly," I said by way of greeting as I sat.

"Not much of an entrance," Molly pouted. "I thought we were having a dramatic moment."

"Thank heavens you've come," I deadpanned.

Molly smiled. "That's better," she said, fishing out a pack of cigarettes and absent-mindedly offering it to me. "Cigarette?"

I took one and stuck it behind my ear. "I'll save it for later," I said. "They're like money in the joint."

Molly smiled and shook her head. She lit one herself. If she remained true to form she would barely smoke it, but would make extensive use of it as a conversation prop, punctuating her sentences with tiny gestures. Molly liked props. She liked anything that made it tough to look away from her. She wasn't needy, but she was the star of the show wherever she went, and she liked it that way just fine.

She took off her glasses and considered me. The glasses were also a prop. I was pretty sure they served no function. She used them in court to quickly transform herself from attractive lady lawyer to smoky-eyed "Bedroom Molly". I had seen the impact the move had on jurors, witnesses, even judges, and it was a sight to behold. But it was all theatrics, and at this point I wasn't even sure that Molly was aware of her moves. I admire tricks, but dislike tics, and had spent enough time with Molly Cameron that I wasn't sure which were which anymore.

"So," she said, "how is jail?"

"They don't think a holding cell is going to put a scare in me, do they?"

Molly considered this. "They probably do," she said. "But that doesn't mean you have to go out of your way to sit in it forever, just to show 'em."

"They want me to name my client," I said.

She nodded. "Yes," she said. "So let's get on that and get you home."

I shook my head. "Molly, my clients pay for confidentiality."

"Sweet-knees," she began, "I have a general idea of what you make. If your clients expect you to be held indefinitely as a material witness to a homicide, they need to give their pretty heads a shake."

"Material witness?" I protested. "I didn't see a thing!"

Molly looked at me as if I were a fluffy kitten that had just done something adorable. "And that isn't what material witness really means, and you know it isn't. You know something. They know you know something. Tell them what it is and get out of this mess."

"I can't believe I'm hearing this," I said. "Would you just rat out a client?"

"First of all, it would only be ratting out a client if your client did the actual killing, which as we have discussed, you do not actually know."

"Molly-," I began.

"Secondly," she said running right over me as if I were a punk in the witness box, "I can't tell you the number of clients that I would love to 'rat out'. I could tell secrets for days, and if I could I'd start with yours and move on to clients who actually have real problems. I am forbidden to do so because of the sanctity of the lawyer-client relationship."

"Tell the truth," I said, "how many of your relationships actually involve any form of sanctity?"

"Oh," she purred, changing gears more smoothly than the new Desoto, "is it girl talk now? I'm game. What's the story on your partner?"

My brows knit. I was going to have to stop doing that. My mother said it causes wrinkles. Which meant somehow I was going to have to convince the world at large to stop asking me stupid questions. And good luck with that.

"I work alone," I said. "You know that."

"Sure, sure," Molly said with a toss of her hair and a coquettish gesture with her cigarette. "I mean the other detective. The one you were palling around with. Fumbling in the dark with loaded firearms. All very naughty. What's his story?"

I shuddered briefly as an unbidden image of Molly Cameron wasting her considerable talents on Jack Justice sprang to mind. "First of all," I said, squeezing my eyes shut tight to try and banish the horror from my mind's eye, "I wasn't working with him, I was on my way to kill him."

"Okay," Molly said, making notes, "let's leave that that out of your statement."

"I'm not making a statement," I said. "And secondly, eww."

She shrugged. "You sure the lady isn't protesting too much?"

I frowned again. "What is that supposed to mean?"

"It means we're friends," she said. "And if you don't happen to shoot the private eye with the lantern jaw, I fully intend to teach him a lesson I sorely need. Are you suggesting my way is clear?"

"Oh my God, Molly," I said. "Isn't there a circus in town or something? Couldn't you just kidnap a monkey?"

"The maxim of law is 'silence gives consent'. Going once, going twice…"

"Sold to the deeply misguided girl attorney," I said.

She shrugged again and played with her cigarette, thoroughly pleased, or at least with confidence that she shortly would be. Was I missing something here?

"Look," I said, "if we could postpone plans for date night and just get me out of here, that would be swell."

"Kitten," she said, "you can walk out of here any time you want. Tell Sabien who your client is and what you were doing across the street from a soon-to-be crime scene. He'll cuss you out for a while and let you go."

"You're sure about that, are you?" I said.

"Did you kill Janet Timms?" she asked.

"Don't be stupid," I said.

"Then I'm sure. Sabien doesn't want you. Well, allow me to rephrase, because simple logic dictates that he must, and badly too."

"Again with the traumatic mental pictures," I protested. "Molly, how is it going to look if I turn in my client? People who come to me expect me to keep their secrets."

Molly Cameron shook her head. "A principled hellcat," she said. "I may have to revoke your blazer badge and secret handshake."

"How do you revoke a secret handshake?" I asked, not really wanting to know.

"Shut up," she said. "I have, at your request, paid a call upon your client this morning. She seemed positively giddy at the news."

"That I was in jail?"

"No, Princess," Molly smiled. "That her husband's secret sexpot is extremely dead and that the whole mess is likely to be dragged into the papers, leaving him humiliated and her with ample grounds for divorce."

I thought about this for a moment. It was true.

"She considers the matter closed and has given me a cash payment for your time, including today. You are off the clock, Peaches." Molly smiled.

I grit my teeth a little. "There isn't any way to do this without making it look like I caved, is there?"

Molly seemed surprised. "Do you really care what Sabien thinks of you?" she asked.

"Of course," I said, "I'll be seeing him again. If he thinks he can get what he wants from me by throwing me in a cell, this isn't going to be easier for me. Or any detective he deals with for that matter."

"I wouldn't worry about that part," Molly smiled.

"Why not?" I said crossly. "The sewing circle has enough trouble taking me seriously. This will just add fuel to the fire."

"I doubt that very much, Trixie," she said, her eyes dancing.

"Miss Cameron," I said as if I'd had just about enough of her lip, which was easy because it was true, "think about this just a minute, would you? You think you kicked in the door of an old-boys club? My old boys have guns. Every time I run into one of them he talks to me like he wants to pat me on the head and buy me candy."

"I refuse to believe that is where they really want to pat you," she said.

"Will you please shut up? I hate being out-Trixied, especially when I'm paying for it."

"Fine," she said, returning her glasses to the bridge of her nose and folding her hands very proper. "You're right to worry about the optics in this case. This has everything the papers adore. Sex, betrayal, sex, murder and sex. I'm amazed no one ran a special edition. And the last thing you want is to be anywhere near this story when it breaks. Your client has washed her delicate hands of the whole affair. She has no expectations of you. If you hurry, you can be an irrelevant sidebar item that never makes it anywhere near the papers. Or you can sit in your cell and be the sexy girl detective who was watching the sexy mistress undress while the alleged sex crime occurred. Page one, above the fold. What will that do for business?"

"Molly, were you coming on to me just there?" I deadpanned.

"Dream on, Sport," she grinned. "You always talk like you don't give a damn what men like Jack Justice think of you. So now would be a perfect time to follow through with that."

I sighed. "I don't care what he thinks," I said, "I just hate to see him take satisfaction in being tougher than me."

Molly Cameron laughed and threw her head back as she did so, showing an alarming number of perfect teeth. "I wouldn't worry about that, Trixie. He walked out of here an hour ago."

"He what?" I snapped.

"Made a statement and walked," Molly said, crossing her arms and enjoying my slack-jawed amazement.

"That rat-bastard," I said at last.

"Careful," she said "that is my future temporary chew-toy you are speaking of."

"That smug son of a-"

"Trixie?" Molly was tapping her pencil against her watch. She was either reminding me that I was paying her by the hour, or that the ship might be sailing on my hopes

of keeping out of the papers. Either way, it was a good point. I nodded grimly.

"All right, councilor," I said, "get Sabien in here and tell him I'd like to make a statement."

Chapter Eleven

I heard her before I saw her, which seemed to be her way. It wasn't a good way, and it got people killed, but I wasn't here to offer free advice. I had come in here to try and get the stink of Robbery-Homicide out of my clothes, or at least stop noticing it quite so much. The stomp of the high-heeled boots was distinctive, and they told me Blondie was still twenty feet away. I raised my glass to signal the bartender that I could use another beer. He nodded, but he wasn't exactly looking at me while he did so. I swiveled my bar stool a hundred and eighty degrees and rested my elbows on the bar behind me. Trixie Dixon, Girl Detective, glared daggers at me. She did that a lot.

"You bastard," she said, pointing a long index finger at me.

That didn't seem to be a question, and I wasn't prepared to argue the point, so I didn't say anything. The bartender put my beer down on the bar beside my right arm with a small thump so I would know it was there.

"Thanks, Jimmy," I said.

"I can't believe you would sell out your client like that," she hissed at me.

Now I was confused, and did my best to show it. "You wouldn't be taking the air just now if you hadn't done the same thing, Princess. And my client may have broken a few of the harder-to-keep Commandments, but at least he isn't a blackmailer."

"A what?" She seemed genuinely thrown by this. Or a good liar, which was my bet.

"You heard me," I said. "Not much point trying to shield my client. When the cops heard your story they would have known who you were taking pictures of and why."

"What made you think I would talk first?" she bristled, drawing herself up to her full height, as if that was going to do any good if it came down to it.

"I didn't know and I didn't give a damn," I said. "I knew you'd talk sooner or later, this is a murder investigation now and Sabien takes those pretty seriously. My client may be a louse, but I got the feeling he legitimately had feelings for the girl, beyond the obvious ones. I decided that he wouldn't want me to get in the way of the search for whoever killed her."

"That's a pretty convenient way of looking at things," she said, still lecturing me like my older sister used to. I never liked it then and I didn't like it now.

"Thanks," I said, picking up my beer. "I thought so."

"You don't even know that your client didn't kill Janet Timms," she snapped. "You were too busy trying to kill me to pay attention."

"If I'd been trying to kill you," I said simply, "you'd be dead. And how in the hell do you know who my client is?"

"Sabien told me," she said. "I don't think he meant to, he was in one of his full-throated monologues and it just kind of popped out. He was comparing you to a retarded chimpanzee, by the way."

"Both of us to retarded chimpanzees," I said. "He used the same line with me. I was so traumatized I decided to have a beer."

"Yeah, you were real tough to locate, by the way," she said, her hands on her hips. "Your car is back at your office, and you strike me as too stubborn to take the bus. This is the first bar on the direct route between points 'a' and 'b' that isn't full of off-duty cops."

"All true," I said, "and the fact that I know the bartender by name tells you this has happened to me once or twice before. But I was easy to find because I wasn't trying not to be, and you didn't find me because you were looking for me. You found me because your car is also back at my office, you are also to stubborn to take the bus and you also felt a powerful need to wet your whistle."

There was a small pause. "So?" she said.

"So bring the lady a beer, Jimmy," I said, knowing he had not moved too far away to listen.

"Make it a rye and water," she said.

"You're just a professional contrarian, aren't you?" I said. It sounded like a question, but it wasn't really.

"And don't be confused by the fact that I'm having a drink," she said, stepping up to the bar beside me and taking a seat. "I still hate you."

"I wouldn't have it any other way," I said. "It's been working so well thus far."

We were quiet for a minute, and Jimmy brought her drink and set it down.

"Your lawyer works fast," she said at last.

I nodded. "Sid Adelman," I said. "The best cheap lawyer money can buy. He doesn't waste a lot of time because at any given moment he's billing six different clients. The man's day is a hundred and thirty-six hours long."

She snorted a little and said nothing.

"Sid didn't do anything real clever this time though," I said. "How come yours kept you so long?"

"I sent her on an errand first," she said.

I nodded. Sending your lawyer to talk to your client was an expensive way to handle these things, but sometimes there wasn't any other way. But that wasn't the part of the sentence that stood out.

"Her?" I asked.

"Yep," she answered.

"You just travel in packs, don't you?"

"We go to the ladies' room in groups, too," she said without smiling.

Silence.

"What's her name?" I said for no reason.

"Molly Cameron," she said.

"She any good?" I asked.

"I have a feeling you're about to find out," she said.

"What does that mean?"

"Skip it," she said with a small shudder.

Silence.

"So if you were working for Mayfield," she said at last, "what the hell were you doing at his mistress' place?"

"Looking for you, idiot," I said. "Going back for more that soon, that was sloppy. Though I gotta admit I didn't really expect it."

"Wait," she said, "what?"

"Maybe your client didn't tell you," I said, "but she sent Roger Mayfield one of your snapshots last week. A real eye-opener too. You've got a career as a pornographer if the girl detective thing doesn't work out."

She shook her head three times, as if shaking off multiple urges to punch me in the teeth and stay on the subject at hand. "Wait," she said again, "what?"

"Wow," I said, "I like your interrogation style. Did they teach you that at reform school?"

Her ears went red and there was briefly murder in her eyes, but she shook it off again.

"Roger Mayfield was being blackmailed?" she said.

"Don't pretend you didn't know," I said. "What else could those photos have been for?"

"Okay," she said, "first of all, I've been on this job since yesterday morning. So if somebody caught your client gathering rosebuds while he may, it wasn't me."

That sounded like a line, but I said nothing.

"Secondly, I'm not working for a blackmailer, idiot," she said in disgust. "I take dirty pictures for the same reason you do."

And now it made sense. "Divorce work?"

She nodded and shrugged at the same time, as if to suggest I was a jackass for having to ask, which suddenly seemed true.

"You're working for Anne Mayfield?" I asked.

"Was," she said. "She doesn't see a real future in the affair, what with her husband's girlfriend being extra dead and all. And she figures when the papers get through with this she'll have everything she needs to put him in the poorhouse and keep him there."

"Oh good," I said, "this case needed a revenge angle too. It was getting stale with all the sex and murder."

"That's what Molly said," she said with a nod. "She figures this will be all over the papers and it was a good idea to stay out of them if possible."

"Yeah," I said rubbing my stubbled chin with my index finger absent-mindedly. "Yeah."

"What is it?" she asked.

"What is what?" I replied.

"There's an idea rattling around in that empty head of yours," she said.

"The papers," I said. "Sabien was on about the papers. He got Sid on the same idea. Come clean now and we'll keep you out of the papers."

"Yeah, so?" she asked. "We didn't exactly come off looking like Nobel contenders in that story. And I want my camera back, by the way. Or I'll kill you."

"You need to stop with the 'killing me' stuff," I said, "I'm trying to think."

"I thought I heard gears grinding," she snorted.

"If Sabien had a chance to humiliate me in the papers," I said, "he'd do it. He wouldn't hesitate. He certainly wouldn't use it for bait to get me to give information he thinks is his God-given right."

She looked at me sideways and nodded slowly. She had clearly danced with Sabien before.

"So when he catches us in a particularly stupid story like this," I said, "how come it's the first club out of his bag? Why does it even occur to him?"

"Because he knows the story isn't going to be anywhere near the papers?" Trixie said, picking up the thread.

"And he's already had a call from someone to make damn sure of that," I said.

"Somebody who is also handling the papers directly, I'll bet," she said.

I shook my head. "Roger Mayfield can't buy that kind of clout on a City Planner's salary."

"What's a City Planner?" she asked.

I shrugged. "I guess he plans cities."

"So you don't know," she said with a contemptuous curl of her lip.

"Neither do you," I pointed out.

"Shut up," she said going back to her drink. "What does any of this get us?"

"It means," I said, "that we're sitting in the middle of something bigger than we thought. And I like to stay ahead of the curve."

"What curve?" she asked. "I'm off the case."

"We're Private Detectives," I said. "We're off the case when we say we're off the case. Which is never just when it starts to get interesting. Besides, I'm on a three-day retainer that hasn't quite run out yet."

"Bully for you," she said.

"You could sit in, if you like," I said for reasons passing understanding.

"Why?" she asked. It was a damn good question.

"We only started making sense of this when we stopped shooting and started talking," I said. That was true.

She thought about it for a minute.

"I want to be clear," she said. "I am only agreeing to this because I think it is in the best interests of my business to close out this ribald little tale of adventure looking like something other than a bumbling idiot."

"Granted," I said.

"And because you are the first detective I have talked to for five minutes that didn't try to pick me up," she said.

"This is also true," I said. "It helps that I don't like you very much."

She nodded and we both took a drink.

"You do like girls, don't you?" she asked.

I nodded. "I like girls," I said. "I just can't stand you."

"Perfect," she said, setting her empty glass down with a thump. "Where do we start?"

Chapter Twelve

As it turns out, where we started was with some shut-eye, as far away from each other as common sense would allow. It had, by this time, been a full day, and Square-Jaw favored a fresh start. He didn't seem the bright-eyed and bushy-tailed type, but he had me meet him the next morning across from the Gazette building, in a second-floor coffee shop I never would have noticed if I hadn't been looking for it. He was there when I arrived, with an oversized cup that made him look like a midget and an expression on his face like a yogi in a trance. I wasn't even sure that he could see me when I arrived.

"Are you having a stroke, or is that supposed to be a smile?" I asked.

"Shh," he said, raising two fingers and giving them a small, smooth wave, like a vaudeville hypnotist.

"Why?" I said, baffled. He didn't look hung over. Or at least, no more hung over than he always looked.

"Coffee," he said. "Get some."

I shrugged. I hadn't been getting along with coffee shops lately, but when in Rome. I walked up to the counter and was greeted by a surprisingly seedy-looking little man. I ordered a coffee and he looked at me as if I had just struck him. He slowly pointed at a large chalkboard behind him and I realized to my horror that everything on it was coffee. There had to be a dozen options, all broken down by the point of origin of the beans, as far as I could tell.

"Holy Toledo," I muttered. "Just give me what he's having. But a normal size."

The man shook his head. "Not sure you could handle Jack's blend," he said.

Now he was just bothering me. Coffee was coffee. He must have sensed my irritation.

"I'll get you something nice," he said, and fixed me a slightly smaller bathtub full of whatever it was that ladies

drank in this booby-hatchery. I nearly fell down when he asked me for a quarter, but paid the man and went over to join Flat Top, whose expression had not changed.

"What is this place?" I asked.

"Have you tried your coffee?" he said serenely.

"Jack, I don't want to talk about the stupid coffee," I snapped.

He looked hurt which I didn't know was possible, so I tried the coffee in exasperation. It was pretty outstanding, and I guess my face must have shown it.

"There are four coffee houses of this quality in the city," he said, as though imparting deep wisdom. "Most focus more on the sale of the beans by the bag, but you can, of course, get a cup. This place is directly across from the newspaper offices, and those boys need rocket fuel and plenty of it, so the ratio is reversed. They make an espresso that can speak directly to God on your behalf."

"What's an espresso?" I asked, not really caring. The hurt look came back. "Please tell me we didn't drive across town in the morning rush just so you could talk in riddles like Charlie Chan?"

He smiled. "So solly," he said. "Here come Number One Son now."

I followed his gaze and there at the counter was a large, red-headed man who looked a little rough. My guess was that he had closed the bar downstairs only a few hours before, but maybe he always looked like that. He was getting a tiny cup of something and a giant cup of something else.

"You know him?" I said, still not sure what we were doing here and still not enjoying playing Dr. Watson.

Justice ignored that and called to the big man as he turned. "Hey, Mike!"

The red-headed man looked up quizzically and his eyes settled on Jack.

"Oh, no," he sighed.

"Yep," I said, "at least he knows you."

"Shut up," Jack muttered as he smiled.

The red-headed man looked toward the door and gestured Jack in the direction of a secluded booth by a tiny window that overlooked the street. The man looked at me, a little puzzled as he did so, obviously unsure of what so much talent was doing in a coffee shop with Jack Justice first thing in the morning, something of which I was profoundly uncertain myself just now.

We settled in to the booth, the big man taking the seat from which he was least likely to be spotted from the counter or the door. I wondered if all of Jack's friends were this keen to not be seen with him.

"Mike, this is Trixie Dixon," Jack said. "We're working on the same case."

I liked that. It sounded much better than "working together" for obvious reasons, but he also avoided making any suggestion that I was his little helper, which was what I expected. I made a mental note to kill him quickly and painlessly when the moment finally came.

"Trixie, this is Mike Rogers," Jack said, "ace crime reporter for the Gazette."

"Aw, shucks," Rogers said sarcastically, and threw back whatever was in the tiny cup. He reacted as if whatever it held was something good, and I wondered if this was a secret booze-can of some kind.

"Rough night?" Jack smiled.

"Every night," Rogers grimaced. "You know the story, day isn't over 'till the paper's put to bed, and the paper's not put to bed until the Editor says it is, or the clock runs dry. And then we start it all over again."

"Didn't really see anything that interesting in the crime beat, Mike," Justice said, clearly fishing.

Mike Rogers bit his lip for a while and smiled. Finally he shook his head. "What could you possibly mean, Jack?" he asked. "Like a little bunny rabbit with a hole in

*her head that got put there while she was being watched
by a pair of his and hers peepers? Something like that?"*

*Jack smiled. "Yeah," he said, "something exactly like
that."*

*The reporter shook his head and prepared for a long
pull on his coffee. I took a discreet sip of mine and waited.
"You've got an angel looking out for you, Jack Justice,"
he said. "We're friends and all, but I'd have had to run
that story just the way Sabien pitched it."*

"Sabien?" I said in protest.

*The two baboons I was seated with exchanged a look at
this.*

"She's surprised?" Mike asked.

*Jack shrugged. "I'm a little surprised he made the call
himself."*

*"He don't like you very much, remember?" Rogers
grinned. "I wasn't the first call he made either, he was
very clear about that."*

*"So you would know that every paper in town was
going to tell the ribald tale of Jack Justice and his heroic
incompetence?" For some reason Jack was amused by this
and it was getting on my nerves.*

*Rogers nodded. "And I'm glad I didn't get a look at
you until this morning, Miss Dixon, 'cause I'd have killed
myself when the story got canned if I'd known there were
two Class-A dishes involved."*

*"Thanks, I think," I said. "I have that effect on a lot of
fellas."*

*"You don't know the half of it," Rogers said. "He'd
have been embarrassed, but you'd have had to move to
Topeka. You can only dress up old photos of the victim so
many ways. A new picture of you and those legs every day
would have sold a lot of papers."*

"Again, thank you," I said, not meaning it.

*"No offense," Rogers said with a small gesture of
surrender with his hands. "But I know the newspaper*

business. Murder is most interesting in the first couple of days, which is also when we don't know anything and we have nothing to print. Your little comedy shoot-'em-up would have made decent copy, but if the powers that be sit on this for more than a couple of days, they'll know too much and you'll never make the story. Gams notwithstanding. Besides, with every day that passes, the column inches go down. What people really want to know when someone is murdered is whether of not they'll be next. Few days go by, they realize it isn't a murder spree and they're probably safe and that's the end of fun. Worst case scenario is they solve this before they call off the dogs. Then we get one day of it and it's over."

Jack nodded sagely. *"Appallingly bad taste aside, Mike, what Miss Dixon and I are chiefly interested in at this point is how the story got from Point A, being giant type above the fold to Point B, being not even a half a paragraph below the tidal schedule."*

Rogers smiled. He seemed to do that a lot, in spite of the fact that he was cynical, callous and probably a drunk. I liked him. *"Couldn't say, Jackie,"* he said. *"By the time I wiped the drool off my chin and got to my editor's office the story was already dead. Somebody worked fast and did it on no uncertain terms. My boss wouldn't even listen to me talk about it. Threw me out on my ear and told me to find a real story. As if there were a story more real than this one."*

Jack nodded and said nothing. I shook my head. None of this made sense, so what was the big jerk nodding for? Did he think he was fooling anybody?

Mike Rogers carried on as if prompted, so maybe he was. *"I got back on the line to Sabien to see if he knew what the rumpus was, and by the time I did, it was a dead deal. Somebody had called him off too. You got friends in high places, Jackie?"*

"He doesn't even have friends in low places," I said.

"Shut up," Jack said without a great deal of urgency.

"Make me," I said.

"How long have you two been married?" Rogers grinned.

"Cut it out, Mike, you give me the heebie-jeebies," Jack said before I could.

"All right, schoolgirls," I said, "I think the real question is who would have the kind of reach to put the lid on the press and the cops at the same time?"

They didn't have a whole lot to say to that.

"I'm not sure I buy any single source," Rogers said with a shrug, "but I've been wrong before. Who else is involved?"

"Can't tell you that," I said.

"Sabien didn't tell you?" Jack said with raised eyebrow.

"Nah," Rogers said sadly, "by the time you two walked out of the clink, the story was deader than the lovely Janet Timms."

"What do you know about her?" Jack asked.

Rogers smiled again. "Who are you working for?" he asked.

"If anyone asks, Sabien told you," Jack said.

"For Pete's sake, Jack-," I protested.

"I can't print a thing," Rogers said defensively. "I just want to know if it's worth risking my job to keep digging."

"Roger Mayfield," Jack said. "She's for Mrs. Mayfield."

"Jack, what in the hell are you doing?" I said loud enough that everyone else in the place looked over to see if I was being molested. They seemed disappointed to find that I was not.

Rogers shook his head. "Never heard of a Roger Mayfield," he said.

"No reason why you should," Jack said. "City Planner. Was having it off with the deceased. Thought he

might be being blackmailed by person or persons unknown. Her ladyship was on a divorce job, now made redundant by the whole 'dead mistress' thing."

"Holy cats," I said, "can you even spell confidentiality?"

Jack thought about this for a moment. "Not off the top of my head, no."

Mike Rogers seemed disappointed by this turn of events. "A lousy City Planner?" he said. "How does a civil servant get that kind of pull?"

"Yeah," Jack said, "this is kind of the mystery. Well, that, and the whole 'sexy murder' thing."

Rogers snorted. "I don't really do mystery," he said. "I do murder and mayhem and scandal when I can get it. Mystery is for paperbacks."

"Good to know," Jack said. "What about the girl?"

"A real dish," Rogers said, forgetting or not caring that we had seen her. "We could have had a field day with this."

"Un-huh," said Jack, unamused. "So what's the story?"

"The story like how?" Rogers said. He was not being coy, he just couldn't imagine why we were interested, which to be honest escaped me right now too.

"Like the apartment," Jack said. "My client couldn't have been keeping her in that by himself."

Rogers smiled. "She owns it. Or did, anyway."

"How do you own an apartment?" I asked.

"You spend a reasonable amount of time servicing the carnal needs of one of the city's most prominent gangsters," Rogers said with a polite smile and folded hands, as if discussing a bridge tournament in a church basement. "And when he tires of you, and bear in mind these guys go through girls like I do peanuts, but when he tires of you, if he still has happy memories of you and might like to revisit them from time to time, he retires you.

Buys you something that makes you a little money and keeps you available to him, if not exactly full-time. She owns the building. The apartment and the shop below. She makes a little rent off that, not much, but enough I guess."

Jack and I looked at each other. Did we really want any part of this?

"Who are we talking about, Mike?" Jack said.

"Al Rossetti," Rogers said with a smile.

"I thought he was mostly legit these days," I said.

Rogers looked mildly impressed, which was probably as impressed as he ever got. "The territory between 'mostly legit' and 'all legit' is vast and treacherous," he said poetically. "In general, if you still use the word 'legit', you ain't."

"Would he have had the reach to shut down your editors?" Jack asked.

Rogers shrugged. "If he wanted to, he or somebody in his pocket could do it in a heartbeat. Why would he?"

"Maybe he wants to take care of Janet Timms' killer himself," I offered.

"Maybe," Rogers said, "but no way he could have got to Sabien, so I ain't sure I buy it."

"Yeah," I said.

"Yeah," Jack echoed.

We sat in silence for a moment.

"Good coffee, though," I said.

Chapter Thirteen

"Won't you please sit down?" the little old lady said with a gracious smile. "Can I get either of you anything?"

"We're fine, Stella," Trixie said, "don't trouble yourself."

The apartment was spacious, and largely free from the accumulation of mementos that usually characterizes a visit to grandma's house. Stella Simple might have been somebody's grandma, but you'd have never known it. She was simply but elegantly dressed in clothes that seemed to be of current style without running to the other extreme, the sad old lady who dresses like a young girl. She was fit and full of verve, but was probably about seventy. She slid back a panel in a cabinet and revealed a well-stocked little bar.

"Are you certain?" she said, smiling like the gracious hostess that she had clearly always been. "I do hate to drink alone, but not nearly as much as I'd hate not having one at all."

I smiled at this and she saw me do it. "Mr. Justice?" she asked again.

"Well," I said, "maybe just a small one."

Trixie glared at me for that, but I pretended that I didn't see her, which was almost but not quite as good as really not seeing her. Stella Simple fixed me bourbon and water and a gin and tonic for herself. She handed it to me with a sparkle in her eye.

"I got it right, didn't I?" she asked. "The water probably isn't your usual, but I thought in deference to the hour of the day…" She trailed off a bit, as though fishing. Not needy, but curious.

"You got it just right," I said, because it was true. She smiled at that and motioned for us to sit.

"I have made a life's work out of reading men who think themselves inscrutable," she said, "and it all begins with a drink. Trixie probably told you all about me."

"Trixie told me nothing," I said. "She said that she knew someone we should see, and has been eating her heart out ever since that I haven't asked."

Stella Simple's eyes danced as she looked to Trixie. "I like this one, dear," she said.

"I don't," Trixie said, "so you can have him."

"You're a detective as well, Mr. Justice?" Stella asked. I nodded. "Well, what can you detect about me?"

I looked at Trixie, who shifted in her chair. My guess was that the Stella she knew was much more direct and to the point than this. The Stella on display here was putting on a show, all for my benefit. My guess is that it had nothing to do with me, beyond the fact that I was a man. This is how Stella Simple was when there was a man in the room. Trixie seemed to be used to something else.

I looked back to Stella. "I could pretend to guess, Miss Simple," I said, "but I'd be cheating. You haven't been out of the business for so long that it's forgotten you. Among certain company, Stella Simple's House is still invoked when one wishes to recall the 'good old days'."

She was pleased by this. "How nice," she said. "They must be thinking of the last house, the big one on Walnut Street?" I nodded. "There were more than a few, Mr. Justice. And I was many things before I was a Madam. In my day I was something of an adventuress. But it is nice that they remember."

She smiled and took a genteel sip of her gin and tonic. I caught Trixie's eye and raised an eyebrow, just slightly, by way of handing off to her. She took her cue.

"Stella, we need some help if you can," Trixie said. "We're in the middle of something and trying to get a sense of how deep the water ahead is."

Stella Simple nodded and smiled. "Of course, dear."

"Janet Timms," Trixie said.

"Janet?" Stella asked, surprised. "I thought she was retired."

I gave my head a small, involuntary shake. Stella saw it and smiled.

"Your friend finds the thought of a young thing like Janet Timms being retired absurd," she said.

"It is," I said.

"And he's not my friend," Trixie said.

"How interesting," Stella said, looking from the girl detective, to me, and back to Trixie.

"Janet Timms," Trixie said. "I thought you might have known her, socially. She might have been with Rossetti around the time…" Trixie trailed off.

"Around the time that Mr. Rossetti retired me?" Stella smiled. "No, not quite. But we have met many times." Stella turned her attention back to me. "I imagine that you are aware, Mr. Justice, that Alphonse Rossetti and his associates run the end of town, including prostitution."

I was and I said so.

"It was not always thus," Stella said, a little wistful. "There were always men who thought they ought to be taking in the profits, of course. By cultivating a clientele of influence on both sides of the law, I was always able to remain independent. Fifteen years ago, Al was a very different man. Full of fire, ready to explode upon anyone who stood in his way. And I knew in my heart that I didn't have a lot of years left to run a house. It is a great deal of work. Of management. The Rossettis had the good grace and political savvy to buy me out on generous terms. They kept the house as it was, the girls stayed on. It went downhill, of course, and in time the house was no longer profitable. If your goal is to take as much money out of something that it can possibly be bled for, it won't live long. But they had the whole trade under them by that time, and did damn well by it." She smiled at me again, as if apologetic for talking business. Or maybe for swearing, I wasn't sure.

"And Miss Timms?" Trixie said gently.

"Even in retirement, I was quite the celebrity in certain circles," Stella said modestly, "and once I was retired and living well, I had the time to take advantage of invitations I received. Al is really a very clever man. By being quite publicly friendly with me, the goodwill I had spent a career building became his. He became the big-hearted operator who finally gave dear old Stella a break. Even then he could see the day when he would want to legitimize his operation, and once he was in the bedrooms of power, he had his start. He made sure my friends saw that I was happy, and he did so by means most men like him would never have thought of. By actually keeping me happy. He was the same with dear Janet, when her time came. She was with him for nearly five years, a sweet girl and very devoted, but always with the knowledge that she could never be more to him than a favorite toy. She never made the mistake so many of these girls do of trying to get involved in the operation, or trying to supplant the wife. Janet enjoyed herself and kept to her place. Five years is a very long time for a man like Al Rossetti to keep a girl, and in the end he probably only gave her up for appearances. Can't be seen without the youngest, freshest flower on your arm, you know. But he loved Janet, I'm sure of it, as much as a man like that ever loves anything. He took care of her too. Gave her a building, you know. This was two years ago now, and he had been buying up so many for so long by then that I'm sure he didn't even notice, but still, quite a gesture. She isn't in any sort of trouble, is she?"

"She's dead," Trixie said simply.

A cloud passed over Stella Simple's face and she took a slightly longer pull on her drink, which was still barely touched. Mine was long gone, but I hadn't talked much. She looked at Trixie.

"Are you on the case?" she asked.

"Yes," Trixie answered.

Stella nodded toward me. "With him?"

Trixie sighed and nodded.

"Good," Stella Simple said, straightening herself, as if that settled that.

"Is there any chance that Al Rossetti killed Janet Timms?" I asked. "Or had it done?"

Stella sighed a little. "There is always a chance with a man like Al," she said. "If he needs someone dead, they die. If he sent someone to kill me I would have no right to be surprised. But there would be no reason, and I can't imagine Janet would have given him one either. I just can't imagine."

"Did you see much of her since Rossetti gave her up?" I asked, sensing our audience was drawing to a close.

"A few times," Stella smiled. "She was still invited out from time to time, to some of the larger events. She kept herself well. She had a steady boyfriend for a while, I met him twice. Good for her, I thought, much more her own age than she had ever had with Al."

"What did Rossetti think of that?" Trixie asked.

Stella smiled. "Al had his hands quite full with a little Irish girl as I recall. Didn't last long, that one. And I'm certain that if he had cared to pay a call upon Janet in that time, she would not have objected. Besides, that was a year ago or more."

"Do you remember his name?" I asked. "Anything about him?"

"Oh, Mr. Justice," she smiled, "I'm sure that boy couldn't have harmed a fly. He was an artist of some kind. Maybe a photographer. Lish, I think. Jim Lish. She called him Jimmy."

I looked at Trixie. "Jimmy Lish?" I said. She shook her head. She had never heard of him either.

"You will find out who did this, won't you, Trixie?" Stella asked.

"You don't think Rossetti would mind?" Trixie said, and we all knew the question that was really being asked, and how important the answer was.

Stella bit her lip, but shook her head. "No," she said. "I think he would be grateful."

Chapter Fourteen

The little man was sweaty and nervous. The kind of nervous that makes everybody within thirty feet nervous too. Not the best quality if you choose to work outside the law. Not really the best quality anywhere, but when a day's work has the potential consequences of landing in a cell or worse, projecting a certain Zen-like calm strikes me as the best personality trait that you can have. It certainly is the common thread between all of the most successful operators I have met. This little fella was in no danger of making that list, of that I was fairly certain.

He had been flustered from the moment he opened the door and found ol' Square-Jaw and I in the grimy little hole that he apparently liked to call his "waterfront hideout". Again, a good criminal would try and avoid that kind of nomenclature. It's like putting a sign out front that says "secret lair". I had mentioned this to Jack at the time – he pointed out that a good criminal wouldn't talk to us at all, and a bad criminal would be in the lockup. Somewhere in the vastness in between the two dwelt the little man we had come to pay a call on. Jack had introduced him as Freddie the Finger, much to the little man's displeasure.

"Geeze, Jackie, how many times do I gotta ask you about that?" the little man had said.

"Sorry Frederick," Jack had replied.

"People might get the wrong idea, is all," Freddie had blustered, picking up steam. "They might get the idea that I am in the habit of assisting agents of the Law such as yourself."

"You are," Jack had said, and cut off further debate by pointing out that we had brought sandwiches and six beers, most of which were still unconsumed.

This had placated the little man, or at least shut him up for a while, as he ate with both hands and it didn't leave him a lot of opportunities to speak. He eyed me suspiciously the entire time, as if I might try and grab his

*sandwich away from him at any moment. He reminded me
of a dog that my Aunt Sylvia used to have. I had tried to
like that dog for twelve years and felt nothing but secret,
terrible joy in my heart when it finally died. I decided then
and there not to make the same mistake with Freddie the
Finger. It would be so much easier to start disliking him
now.*

*When at last he could speak again without choking, the
little man looked at Jack just as suspiciously as he had me.
"It is unlike you, Jackie, to bring a girl around to my
hideout," he said.*

*"I didn't," Jack said, "at least not like you think. This
isn't a social call."*

"You're working?" Freddie seemed surprised.

"Shut up," Jack said.

*" I didn't mean it like that," Fred protested, then
looked at me. "He works all the time. Very flush is our
Jackie."*

*"At ease, Mr. The Finger," I said. "We're both on the
same case."*

*"She's a detective?" The little man turned back to Jack
in disbelief.*

*"She is," I said. "Talk about her in the third person
again and you'll need a new nickname, 'cause I'm gonna
break your little hands, Mr. The Finger."*

*"Sorry," he protested, "sorry. I didn't mean nothing by
it. And it's Hawthorne. Fred Hawthorne. The 'finger'
thing is just a nickname, just like Jackie's."*

"Just like Jackie's what?" I asked.

*"Nickname. Black Jack Justice, they call him," the
little man smiled proudly.*

"We don't need to get into that, Fred," Jack said.

*"Wait," I said, "you call yourself Jack Justice, and you
gave that nickname a nickname? Sounds socially
awkward."*

"What is she talking about?" Hawthorne asked, forgetting my threat of a moment ago.

"I've been with her all day," Jack said, "and have only occasionally known."

"Wait... wait...," I said, "are you saying that Jack Justice is your actual name?"

"Well of course it is," Freddie said, astonished. "Who would make something like that up?"

"As opposed to 'Black Jack'," I said, "which has the hallmark of subtlety all over it."

"Ah," Freddie seemed delighted, "there is an interesting story behind that moniker-"

Jack bounced an empty beer can off Freddie's head.

"-which I will relate to you on a different occasion," the little man said without missing a beat.

I looked at Jack. "As much fun as it is to meet your little frat buddy here, Black Jack, can we get down to business so I can get the hell out of here? And be anywhere else?"

"What's wrong with her?" Hawthorne said, referring to me in the third person for the third time. I leaned forward with the intention of breaking just one of his fingers, but Jack caught my eye and shook his head. So I punched Hawthorne solidly in the arm instead.

"Ow!" he protested like a little girl. "Jackie, did you see that?"

"I saw it," Jack sighed.

"Well, make her stop," Freddie whined.

"Make me yourself," I said, popping him another sweet one in the shoulder, which made him squeal even louder.

"Trixie, for God's sake, cut it out," Jack said. "I didn't hit yours, keep your paws off mine."

"Mine was a seventy-year-old lady," I protested.

"It still counts," he said, motioning Freddie to come over and sit by him.

"She's crazy, Jackie," the little man whimpered.

"Yes," Black Jack said simply.

"Just because she's a lady, doesn't mean she can act like that. Not in my own place." Proximity to Jack was making the little guy feel tougher. "I might forget that I'm a gentleman."

"And God knows nobody wants that, Fred," Jack said soothingly. I glared at Freddie and he moved slightly closer to Jack, as if involuntarily. "Now, I don't know how long I can control her, so if you tell us what we need to know, we can get out of your place faster."

The little man looked up at Jack in disbelief. "Is you really playing 'good cop', Jackie?" he asked.

Jack shrugged. "Everything is relative," he said.

Freddie the Finger looked back at me and nodded. "Okay," he said. "Okay, I get you. What do you need?"

Jack opened another beer and handed it to Freddie, who still had an open one in his other hand. He was momentarily flustered by this, but settled quickly into alternating hands, much as he had with the sandwiches.

"Ever hear of a guy named Lish?" Jack asked. "Jimmy Lish?"

"Jimmy Lish?" Freddie seemed surprised. He looked at me cautiously. "Jackie, what kind of case you workin' on here?"

Jack said nothing. Freddie squirmed and looked at me again.

"Freddie," Jack said, "are you a little squeamish about talking about Jimmy Lish in front of Miss Dixon?"

Freddie nodded and took a drink.

"Does Miss Dixon strike you as a particularly delicate flower?" Jack asked. Freddie looked at me again and I took a stomp forward with my right foot, making him jump.

"No," he said. "I guess she ain't. I guess you ain't," he corrected himself quickly and I smiled my second-best smile, which seemed to soothe him.

"Jimmy Lish," Jack said quietly.

"Jimmy Lish," Freddie said, picking up the thread, "is best known in certain circles for... that is... he takes... photographs for certain... gentlemen's magazines."

"He's a pornographer," I said simply.

"Okay," said Freddie, surprised, "yes, he is that. What you said, yes he does. Is, I mean. No offense."

"None taken," I said.

"We heard he was a photographer," Jack said. "An artist."

"Sure, Jackie," Freddie snorted, "the kind of art they keep behind the counter and sell you wrapped up in brown paper." This seemed to amuse him a great deal, until he remembered that I was in the room and became uncomfortable again.

"Where can we find him?" Jack asked.

"I think he used to have a studio over on Jacob. Near the St. Pete," Freddie said. "But he ain't always there. This... um... trade of his, it is actually kind of a hobby."

"He should try macramé," I suggested. "It's all the rage."

"No," Freddie said seriously, "I do not think that Lish would enjoy that as much as he does the other thing. He likes his fun but it don't pay, not enough. And he ain't the sort with the patience for portrait sittin'. So he makes most of his money on the side."

"He's a blackmailer," Jack said simply.

Freddie shrugged. "I do not know him well, but this is what I hear," he said. "I give him a wide berth, myself. He is not a very nice man."

"Freddie doesn't trust blackmailers," Jack told me.

"He does not," Fred agreed.

"Wise foreign policy," I said, and Hawthorne beamed at this.

"Jacob, by the St. Pete?" Jack asked.

"Yes, sir," Freddie said, taking a pull on his beer and clearly feeling that the interview may be done.

"One more thing," Jack said.

"Name it," Freddie said with an expansive gesture.

"Al Rossetti," Jack said.

Freddie's face fell, hard.

"I got not one word to say on such a subject as that," Freddie said.

"Don't get hysterical," Jack said.

"No, seriously Jackie, you come into my place when I ain't even here-"

"You gave me a key," Jack deadpanned.

"Well," Freddie paused, "leaving aside for the moment that this is an interesting point-"

"Thank you," said Jack.

"You bring in a person whom I do not know," Freddie said gesturing towards me and raising his hands defensively as he realized that he had done it again. "And you ask me about one of the biggest gangsters in town, whom I have just remembered that I have never heard of."

"Freddie," Jack interrupted, "please, just breathe a little, okay?"

"I would like to Jackie," the little man whimpered, "but you do not make it very easy on me, you know that?"

"Freddie," Jack said, "Miss Dixon and myself are in the middle of something, is all. And if it were to turn out quite suddenly that the Rossetti family was also in the middle of that same something, it could be very uncomfortable for all involved, could it not?"

Freddie nodded.

"So if you were to let us know that, and we were, as a result, able to reassess our involvement in this matter, you would actually be helping Al Rossetti, would you not?"

Freddie breathed a little. "There really isn't a lot I can tell you, Jackie. Rossetti is mostly legit these days."

"Mostly legit," I offered, "is somewhat crooked, yes?"

Freddie whimpered. "Mostly legit on the way to bein' all legit," he said. "Big Al has been workin' at it for years.

They say all he needs to do is find a way to clean the money and he's out."

"How do his troops feel about this?" Jack asked.

"They worry," Freddie shrugged. "What working guy wouldn't? The soldiers, they'd catch on somewhere, but the bigger fish, they'll have to go legit with the company. No other operator would trust them. But nobody would ever cross Rossetti."

"Who's Big Al's number two?" Jack asked.

"Brazzi," Freddie said. "Anthony Brazzi. Why?"

"No reason," Jack said. He looked at me.

"You still in?" he asked.

"What, you think I'm gonna have an accident like your little friend here?" I snorted. Freddie looked hurt.

"If you are," Jack said, "now would be the time to let me know."

"We got nothin' on Rossetti anyway," I said, "beyond one count of being Al Rossetti and one count of suspicion of being Al Rossetti."

"That's about it, all right," Jack nodded. "And Jimmy Lish is in here somewhere."

"So get your hat, Black Jack," I said, "and let's go see a man about some dirty pictures."

Chapter Fifteen

Jimmy Lish's place was on the second floor of a walk-up above a dry cleaners, which had closed at five-thirty. The sign on the door was tastefully lettered, *"James P. Lish, Photography. Appointments only"*. It was a nice job, and made the person reading it begin to forget the narrow wooden steps they had just climbed, or the smell of solvents that crept up from the first floor. He had certainly paid more for it than he did for the lock on the door, which was thirty years old if it was a day and would have taken me no more than six seconds to get past if it had actually been locked.

As I pushed the door gently open I looked at Trixie and she pulled the Beretta from her handbag. It wasn't the most reliable handgun on the planet, and I suspected that she had selected it because it looked nice, but it did and I wasn't prepared to argue the point.

We crept into the office and saw immediately that Jimmy Lish might be a smut peddler and a blackmailer, but nobody was going to mistake him for a housekeeper. There were loose papers everywhere, and several of the drawers on the row of filing cabinets were left hanging open. The smell was actually stronger.

"I don't know how he stands it in here," I said.

Trixie stepped over to the window and pried it open. "That's not the cleaners," she said, "that's gasoline."

"How can you tell?" I said, sniffing the air.

"If you had your suit cleaned more than once a year, you'd know the difference," she said. "Get the light."

The office looked worse under illumination. This place was not just a naturally occurring mess.

"It's been tossed," I said.

"Ya think?" Trixie said, looking at the desktop. "No appointments today," she said.

"Oh, good," I said, pulling the handle of a cabinet drawer that was hanging half-open. It was empty but for a couple of unused file-folders. "Some of these have been cleaned out," I said, "and recently."

"How come 'recently'?" Trixie asked, going through the desk drawers.

"No dust," I said, opening more drawers and finding several in which the files had clearly been taken apart and shoved back into the drawers. "Somebody was looking for something."

"Well," Trixie said, "if it was in Lish's desk, my guess is they found it. No soap over here."

"What about a phone book? Addresses, that kind of thing," I asked.

"Gosh, Jack, I never would have thought to look for that," she said, moving toward the files.

"Don't get lippy," I said.

"Born that way, Peaches," she said, going over the same ground I just had.

"I just looked in there," I said.

"And now I'm looking," she said. "Go hard-boil something."

I moved down the row of filing cabinets. More drawers were askew, more flies had been mauled. Some things looked to have been taken, but it was tough to say what, or why. I opened one of the folders and found some very tasteful studies of a brunette who didn't look to be too much older than not nearly old enough for this.

"What have you got?" Trixie asked.

"Lish's hobby job," I said. "Some sunbathing pictures, and signed release from the girl."

"Those were shot inside," Trixie said, at my elbow now. "Probably right here."

"So?" I asked.

"So she isn't sunbathing."

"It's a euphemism," I said.

"I know what it is," she said. "It's also stupid."

She pulled out a stack of prints from the next file. "Hello," she said, neither surprised nor embarrassed. "These ones are a lot less artistic."

I looked over her shoulder. It was true. "Same girl," I said grimly, pulling the release from the new file. "Six months later," I remarked.

"Slippery slope?" Trixie asked.

"Something like that," I said.

"What does it say her name is?" Trixie asked.

"Why?"

"Because if two sessions six months apart are beside each other, these aren't organized by date," she said. "So maybe name?"

"Karen Mitchell," I said without looking, having read it already. I replaced the files.

"M for Mitchell," Trixie said. "So T would be this way?"

"T for Timms?" I asked.

"Now you're thinking," she said. "At last."

She followed the row of cabinets to the logical area and began searching. I moved in the opposite direction. The smell of gasoline got stronger. There were two drawers in the bottom row that were wide open. I knelt beside them and, sure enough, that's where the smell was coming from. The contents of the files were mostly ruined, as if someone had poured liquid all over them.

"Hell," I heard Trixie say.

"Find something?" I asked without looking.

"Yeah," she said, "I found a big suspicious nothing."

"Explain," I said, noticing a cigarette that had been dropped on the floor by the cabinet and allowed to burn out. The ash was an inch long and I left it undisturbed.

"If there were files on Janet Timms," Trixie said, "they've been cleaned out. And from the size of the hole she left in the files, there must have been a hell of a lot of them."

"She was with the guy for a while," I said, pushing my hat back on my head as I surveyed the situation. "Looks like she was into at least one of his hobbies."

"Think she was into the blackmail too?" Trixie asked. "I can't find anything that looks like Lish's 'work' pictures, but they might have been cleaned out too."

"If you were a blackmailer," I offered, "would you keep your bread and butter in a studio with your name on the door?"

"I would not," she said, "but I am not an idiot, and I have not yet established that we can say the same about Jimmy Lish."

"Point taken," I said.

"What have you got?" Trixie said, looking over my shoulder.

"These two drawers have been doused with gas. Like somebody realized they couldn't take everything away, and they couldn't search all of it, and they wanted to get rid of it." I pointed to the cigarette on the floor. "They poured the gas, dropped a smoke and bolted."

"I don't blame them," Trixie said. "This place would go up like a tinderbox."

"Or not at all," I said, standing up. "By the time they got down the steps and across the street, they must have realized that nothing was happening in here."

Trixie nodded. "If it was gonna burn," she said, "it would have happened fast."

"So why didn't they come back and finish the job?" I asked.

"Better part of valor time?" she offered.

"Sure," I said, "but why? You break into an office, you turn it upside down. You take as many files as you can carry, including any picture that might include our murder victim, but you can never take it all, and you can't be sure there aren't more pictures of Timms in this mess."

"So you burn it," Trixie said. "I get it."

I shook my head. "You think they brought gasoline up with them? I mean, in the first place?"

Trixie thought about that. "There's a station at the end of the street," she said. "Or maybe they had a jerry-can in their car."

"Okay," I said, "so they're taking some time here. They're clearly not worried that someone is on to them about the break-in. But when the fire doesn't take, they don't come back in."

Trixie shrugged. "Maybe they didn't stick around," she offered.

"Yeah, but why not?" I asked. Something wasn't right. Something didn't fit. People did things for a reason, and if you couldn't follow the line of thought, you were missing something.

"Maybe they were just here to help themselves to some smut," Trixie said. "The Janet Timms collection wouldn't be a bad choice."

"You know that's not it," I said, looking around the room. The far end of the room was open space, clearly that was the "studio". To the side there was a small counter with some photographic equipment, a coffeepot and a hotplate. All the comforts of home. I could see an open door at the end of the hall, and the plumbing fixtures made it obvious it was the bathroom. There was one door unaccounted for.

"What do you think that is?" I asked, pointing at it.

Trixie shrugged. "Closet?"

"There's a light bulb over the door," I said.

"Okay, genius, it's a darkroom," she sighed. "A photographer has a darkroom."

"The door is closed," I said, walking over to it, "and the light isn't on."

"I have no idea what you're driving at," she said, following me. "If your psychic powers are failing you, why don't you open the damn door and take a look?"

I opened the damn door and took a look.

"Aw, hell," Trixie breathed.

Inside the darkroom was a tall, wiry man, curled on the floor, very dead.

"Jimmy Lish?" she asked.

"My guess," I said.

"How long, do you think?" She was no shrinking violet. The smell in here was worse than any in the office, but she toughed it out.

"Maybe early this morning," I said. "Maybe longer. Looks like a .38."

"So our mystery guest comes in, he looks around," she began.

"Or they," I offered. "My bet is two."

She shrugged. "So they come in, they look around, they start cleaning out the files."

I chimed in. "They take anything they can find on Janet Timms."

"And who knows what else," she added.

"But it's too much to search, and they can't be sure. And they need to be sure."

She frowned. "Why do you say that?" she asked.

"Because of what happened next," I said.

She nodded and held her hand up as if to acknowledge the stupid question. "They decide to burn the place down. Subtle. You think it's Rossetti?"

"I think it's his boys," I said. "That's why I'm thinking there's two. One goes to get some gas. Maybe he's back, maybe he's not, but Lish barges in and gets himself dead."

Trixie took over. "A gunshot. Now they have to hurry. But they're a little bit stupid and a little bit cowardly, so they don't set the fire going. They throw down a smoke and hope it works like it does in the pictures. It all hangs nice and neat."

"Yeah," I said. "Except Lish was the closest thing we had to a lead. And it gets worse."

Trixie nodded. "Now it's for the Law," she said.

Chapter Sixteen

Lieutenant Sabien was not happy. His own men scampered out of his way like bunnies in the path of a bulldozer. Black Jack and I were once again on the same side of an interview table at Robbery-Homicide, though this time nobody had bothered to cuff us, either because we were not actually suspects, which was possible, or because Jack's handcuff trick was starting to embarrass them, which seemed more likely.

"Two corpses in two days is a bit much, even from you, Justice," the good Lieutenant barked, his lips curled around the remnants of his cigar which appeared to have been extinguished hours earlier.

"Hey," I chimed in, "it's a personal best for me."

"You shut up now," Sabien growled while he paced the floor on the other side of the table. When he got like this I liked to imagine him in a giant bear suit. It amused me and I could tell that it confused and annoyed him.

"To be fair, Lieutenant," Jack said, "the first corpse doesn't really count. I was just nearby when it dropped, I didn't actually discover it. For which I blame her."

"And I blame you," I said.

"Right," Jack continued, "it's still an open point. Best not to bring it up at all."

"I'm gonna bring the both of you up," Sabien glared, "on any charge I can think of, just to get you off the street."

"Such as what?" I protested. "Gross competence? Aiding and abetting the pursuit of law and order?"

"How about the Break&Enter at Lish's studio?" Sabien said, his palms flat on the table, glaring at me.

"There was no Break," Jack said, leaning back in his chair, "there was only Enter. Is that even a crime?"

"Actually," I said quietly, as if in an aside, "I think it is."

Jack was silent for a moment. "Really?" he asked.

"Pretty sure," I nodded.

Jack considered this. "I should really stop using that line," he said.

Sabien's rage had settled into a nice, quiet seethe as he regarded us. "What is this?" he asked in horror. "You two making some cozy time now?"

"No," Jack and I said in unison.

"You owe me a Coke," Jack said quietly to me.

Sabien slammed his fist upon the table.

"Damn it, this is serious!" he bellowed. "You two are up to your necks in this, and if you want to see the light of day anytime soon, you will stop with the Amos and Andy routine and I mean now!"

"Amos and Andy?" I said, legitimately confused.

"I think he means Burns and Allen," Jack offered helpfully.

"What about the Bickersons?" I suggested.

Jack smiled as if he had completely forgotten about Sabien. "I love that show," he said.

Sabien's face went purple with rage, and he slammed the table and took in a long breath, as if preparing for one of his epic tirades.

"One second, Kingfish," Jack smiled, "we'll be right with you."

"Nelson!" Sabien hollered at no one we could see. "Book these two on suspicion and get them out of my face!"

There was a small pause. The door did not open.

"Nelson!" Sabien bellowed again, louder, but with the same result.

"Good help is hard to find," Jack said with a sad shake of his head.

Sabien sat heavily in the chair opposite us and grasped both his temples at once with his great, meaty left hand.

"What is it you two want?" he said, his voice lower. "What are you after?"

"Protecting the interests of our clients," I said.

"You don't have a client," Sabien glared at me. "Anne Mayfield paid you off and closed the books."

"Why Lieutenant," I snapped, "you haven't been eavesdropping on attorney-client interviews, have you?"

Sabien flushed. "She told us when she made a statement," he said testily. "We have actually been speaking to the principals in this case, you know. On account of the fact that this is the Homicide division."

"Speaking as a taxpayer," Jack said, "I'm delighted."

"I don't think you understand," Sabien said, as if explaining himself to a guinea pig, or perhaps a ham and cheese on rye. "That means that it is we who investigate murders. We. Not you. You peek in windows and spy on housewives and do whatever else we can't be bothered to do."

"I haven't followed a housewife in days," I said.

"I have," Jack said, "but just to stay in practice. Those little vixens are cunning."

"Again with the wise routine," Sabien wailed as if he were a moose with a toothache. "How about I tell the papers what you two comedians were doing while Janet Timms was being murdered?"

Jack leaned forward in his chair as if this were what he had been waiting for, and it probably was. "That's a load, and you know that it is," he said. "You dangled the story in front of I don't know how many newshawks, and then you got a phone call from somewhere, didn't you? Keep the whole thing quiet, or else."

Sabien seethed and muttered under his breath. "Rogers," he said.

"You leave him out of this," Jack said. "You called him because you knew we were friends and you knew he'd run it anyway and you knew that he'd tell me it was you that sent him the lead."

"Shaddup," Sabien sulked.

"Who was it, Sabien?" I chimed in. "Who called you off?"

"Nobody calls me off!" Sabien barked. "The Timms murder will get solved all right. It just gets kept quiet while it does."

Jack shook his head. "And you don't find that suspicious?"

"It don't matter what I find it," Sabien said crossly. "It is what it is, and it's tough enough solving a murder while you tiptoe through the tulips. So if you two could stop dropping bodies in my lap, that would be swell."

Jack leaned a little further forward. Any more and he'd be laying on the table. "Sabien, did you even stop to wonder how the story stayed out of the papers?"

Sabien's brow furrowed. "What do you mean? You know how," he said. "Word came down the ladder."

"Right," I said. "That's what stopped you from talking any more. But the cat was already out of the bag. So what kept it out of every paper in town?"

"I didn't call every paper in town," Sabien said. "Mike Rogers was my first call."

"You were gonna give him an exclusive," Jack smiled, "and tell him everybody was running it."

Sabien grinned back at Jack. "Salt in the wound," he said.

Jack shook his head. "The question still stands, Sabien," he said. "You think you have enough pull to kill a story like that? You think Mike Rogers would just drop it 'cause you said so?"

Sabien paused, as if something were sinking through the first few layers of his thick skull. "What are you saying?"

"Somebody got to the Gazette editors," I offered. "And we're betting it isn't the same person."

"Or the same side of the law," Jack said, leaning back in his chair.

   Sabien considered this and waved his hand dismissively. "Cut it out," he said. "Lish and Timms were running a blackmail scheme, maybe more than a few. One of their victims must have caught up with them. We'll find out who, and when we have proof, it won't matter who they know." This last part was a veiled threat toward Jack. Roger Mayfield was clearly still suspect number one.

   "That's a nice theory," Jack said. "It might even be right. Or maybe Janet Timms stole her back catalogue from Jimmy Lish, who then shot her in reprisal."

   "And then returned to his studio," I offered, "where in despair at what he had done, he shot himself in the face."

   "And then hid the gun," Jack added.

   "And tried to burn the place down to cover his crime," I said, warming to the theme.

   "Nelson!" Sabien bellowed again to no effect.

   "Who's Nelson?" I asked Jack.

   He shrugged. "No idea," he said, "but I wouldn't want to be him."

   "Just get the hell out of here," Sabien said, raising his hands slightly in the direction of heaven and shaking them as if making a strong request of whoever lived there. "Get out of here and stay out of this case! You hear me? No more bodies!"

   "Sabien," Jack said, rising to his feet, "Jimmy Lish didn't get more dead because we found him. It was just basic detective work. You might even have got around to it eventually."

   "Out!" Sabien bellowed. "Out and stay out!"

   "Come on, Gracie," Black Jack said. "I know when we're not wanted."

Chapter Seventeen

By the time we hit the street it was too late to do anything useful, so Trixie flagged a cab and told me to meet her in the morning at 36 Wellington Avenue.

"That's right downtown," I said.

"Yes it is," she said, climbing into the taxicab.

"What is that?" I said out loud. I knew the block, but I was drawing a blank.

"I'll see you there at nine," she said.

"I have to get my car from Lish's," I said. The good Lieutenant had once again arranged a lift for us in the back of a squad car, leaving me stranded.

"Then I guess you'll have to get up extra early," she said, not understanding me.

She closed the door before I could protest further and was gone. I looked at my wristwatch. Ten-fifteen. Never let it be said that the cops didn't know how to waste my time. I hoofed it north toward my apartment, where I would buy myself a drink and call it a day. It took a while to get there, so I made it two. Or possibly five.

I hate getting up at the same time as everybody else. Whatever I'd consumed the night before, it wasn't enough to keep me in bed. I would have been prepared to swear that I had drank less than the decline in the level of brown liquid left in the bottle might suggest, but since I was resolutely alone, my best alternate theory is that I was plagued by alcoholic shoemaker's elves. Which seemed somehow unlikely. The point is that I didn't have a real hangover, and that wasn't why I hated getting up at that hour. Getting up was fine. Being up, going anywhere at the same time that the rest of the city was going somewhere else, that was my problem.

Early, late, didn't matter much to me, I just disliked breaking stride constantly to keep from knocking people over, and for some reason the general populace was too self-involved to scamper obligingly out of my way. Maybe it was because it was a work day and they were all in character, ready to play whomever they were supposed to be. They were important, and I was not frightening enough to break them from that comfortable illusion. Perhaps I should invest in an eyepatch. Hell, a blunderbuss wouldn't have been enough to buy me a little space on the crosstown bus at that hour.

At last I was back in the relative isolation of my car, and made my way stop and go right into the heart of the city. 28 Wellington was the Federal Building, and through some miracle there was a space out front, so I parked and walked towards Delaware. After a minute I saw Trixie eating a hot dog and looking annoyed.

"You're late," she said.

"Yeah, but we both expected that," I said. "You only said nine o'clock so I'd be thirty-seven minutes late and you could complain when I walked up instead of saying good morning."

She paused for a moment, though I wasn't sure if she was thinking or just chewing.

"Good morning," she said at last.

"Was that so hard?" I smiled.

"You're late," she said.

"I can't believe you're eating that," I said. "It's nine in the morning."

"It's nine thirty-seven in the morning," she said with her mouth full.

"My point stands," I said.

She shrugged. "This is when they're fresh. Have one."

I shook my head. "Black coffee, rye toast and a boiled egg."

"I don't think he makes that," she said with a glance at the vendor who had sold her breakfast, whom she caught with his eyes on her backside. Was it nine in the morning to no one but me?

"No," I said, "I mean-"

"I know what you mean," she said, "I just don't give a damn. Let's get at it." She turned and began to climb a large set of stairs towards a big, grey slab of a building.

"Get at what?" I asked.

"We're here," she said, pointing at the building.

To my deep and obvious disgust, it was the Central Branch of the Public Library.

"36 Wellington," I said.

"That's right," she said, heading up the stairs.

"Why didn't you just tell me to meet you at the library?" I asked, following her.

"Because I wanted to see the look on your face," she said, "and I didn't really feel like an argument last night. We need answers, 'cause right now, we don't even know what the questions are."

"Such as what?" I asked. There were a lot of stairs. I realized that I was mimicking the girl detective's run, which had her stepping on every stair in rapid succession. Made sense if you were wearing heels and a skirt, I guess. I went back to my normal style of walking up, taking three steps at a time, and it felt better.

We reached the top of the long staircase and Trixie grimaced with her hand on her side. "Remind me not to go for a run right after I slam down a frankfurter," she said.

"I'm not sure how often that's going to come up," I said, "but I'll try and remember."

Trixie threw open the main doors and spoke in hushed but still urgent tones. "So I got to thinking last night, while you and Sabien were barking at each other – the real mystery here is how this whole mess has been kept out of the papers."

"Well," I said, "that, and the whole 'double homicide' thing."

"Details," she said with a wave of her hand as she headed down some steps from the main lobby. The stairs circled around gently as they carved their way into the bowels of the building. Where in the hell were we going?

"The point is, we think somebody at City Hall started the chain of calls that shut down Sabien, right?"

"Sure," I said, not caring.

"So even if the calls from the other side of the law did come from Rossetti, which we don't really know," she said, "and even if they were only related to Janet Timms' status as Rossetti's ex-chew toy, which we don't know, someone important intervened on behalf of your client."

"Maybe," I said.

Trixie stopped her descent for a moment and considered this. "Okay," she said, moving again. "Maybe. But it seems likely. He does work there."

"This I grant you," I said.

We reached the bottom of the steps and she flung open a door marked, *"Periodical Archives"*.

"So it's a murder investigation," Trixie said, "and it involves a sexy mistress. And your boy is a suspect. Even if he's not guilty it could be embarrassing, and remember, City Hall is a place where people try very hard to avoid being attached to a scandal since public opinion can result in them losing their job."

"So?" I was working hard to maintain the illusion that I was completely disinterested in this train of thought, but it was starting to make a certain amount of sense.

"So let's say you're somebody important. It's a stretch, but just pretend," she said. "If you intercede on Roger Mayfield's behalf, you could be putting your career in serious jeopardy. Remember, you're calling off the police, or at least getting them to keep their mouths shut, but you can't call off the papers. Somebody else is doing that, and you might not even know it's happening."

I thought about this. "So by putting the reins on Sabien," I said, "I'm risking connecting myself or my bosses to a messy public relations disaster that might be about to happen anyway."

"Yes," Trixie said, smiling.

"So why am I doing that for little old Roger Mayfield?" I asked.

"It's an interesting question," she said.

"So let's go ask him," I said.

"Don't be stupid," she said. "He won't tell you."

"Then let's ask somebody else," I shrugged.

"No one is going to talk to us, Jack," she said.

"Not if we don't try," I said.

"We need to know what is going on," she said, "and that means finding out what Roger Mayfield is really working on, and therefore why he is so important to somebody, or a small group of somebodies."

She stopped at a set of drawers and pulled one open. "Microcards," she said.

"I know what they are," I said.

She ignored this. "These contain tiny photographs of newspapers which we can read with the aid of those machines over there."

"I know what they are," I repeated.

"In the front of every newspaper," she said heading toward the machines with a small pile of microcards, "there is a whole section that has nothing whatsoever to do with sports."

"I know it," I said. "Sometimes they put the puzzle there."

"Nice," she said. "They also put stories on public matters such as those which occur in and around City Hall in there. And we are going to read them."

"Why?" I asked, knowing the answer but hoping for her to slip up and give me something to base a counter-argument on.

"Because I said so," she said simply. That was the end of that.

"What are we supposed to be looking for?" I protested.

"The name 'Roger Mayfield' or the words 'City Planner' would be a place to start. You might want to keep notes about what city issues are dealt with on which card number," she said, "so you can find them again later when we know which story we're actually interested in."

"I'm not interested in any of them," I said.

"Fine," she said. "But this is the boring part. This is where we scan every paper looking for where to start. It'll go much faster if we both look. After that, if you're still stupid, you can bring me trays when I ask for them."

"I don't like you very much," I reminded her.

"Excellent," she said, "I was afraid I might be slipping."

It took two and a half hours to find any lateral reference to my client in the archives. Politicians make the papers, civil servants are supposed to be invisible. This was the worst part, scanning card after card, suddenly realizing that I had no memory of the previous eight minutes and wondering if I had missed what we were looking for in the process. Finally his name popped in an article on a public meeting with a Riverton Resident's Association, which I was surprised to learn existed. It was just a sidebar, but Roger Mayfield of the City Planner's office was to be one of several speakers at the meeting to deal with concerns about the Long Branch Expressway project, of which Mayfield was the Chief Planner.

And so began stage two, in which Trixie read everything that the papers had to say about the Long Branch. This seemed a little unnecessary. It was an expressway; they were popping up all over the country. Supposed to make it easier for folks who had moved their two-point-five kids out to the sticks to get back in to the city for work and play. Supposed to guarantee prosperity for generations to come. Rah-rah stuff. I had heard the talk, mostly at the barber shop. But there was no dissuading her once she was going. I shuttled trays of cards back and forth for a while before being replaced by an earnest male librarian in a cardigan who seemed to know Trixie and eyed me with dismay. He offered his expert advice and brought things much more quickly that I did, and then stood quietly beside her while she stared into the card reader, undressing her with his eyes with a religious fervency. His desperation was palpable and seemed destined to end in disappointment, but I elected to give him some space and took a small nap at an unoccupied reading table under a copy of a hopelessly out-of-date foreign periodical.

I awoke to the sudden removal of the newspaper from my face three hours later.

"Okay," she said.

"What did I miss?" I asked. "Did Poindexter get lucky?"

She smiled in spite of herself. "He did not. He's much too useful in his current state of agitation."

"That's tough but fair," I said, stretching. "What do we know?"

"Roger Mayfield is the lead pencil-pusher on the Long Branch project," she said, "which has gone in a hurry from 'theoretical plan for the city of tomorrow' to 'about to happen'. A big hurry."

"How did that happen?" I asked.

"It's an election year," she said. "Federal politicians like to have their pictures taken in front of bulldozers."

"So the money started flowing," I said.

"Both taps on full," she said.

"That makes things interesting," I said.

"It does, doesn't it, Sleeping Beauty?" she asked.

"Any reason for somebody at City Hall to think that Mayfield being arrested for the murder of his nubile and very willing ex-gangster's moll of a mistress can derail this deal?"

Trixie shook her head. "Nothing can derail this deal," she said. "It's a monster."

"So we're back to zero?" I asked.

She shrugged. "The Riverton thing is bugging me," she said.

I blinked at her. "Pretend that I wasn't paying any attention," I said.

She frowned. "The route of the expressway has been planned for years. A straight run into the city and right into the heart of downtown. Keep the cars running at full speed the whole way, that's the idea."

"So what does that have to do with Riverton?" I asked. Riverton was a poor neighborhood about twenty blocks to the west. No one driving in from anywhere wanted to go to Riverton.

"In the last six months the map's been re-drawn," she said. "Right around the time that federal money started to flow. The Long Branch now comes up straight into Riverton."

I shook my head. Maybe I was still just sleepy. "And dumps off an expressway full of cars into crosstown traffic?"

"Yeah, this was the question," Trixie nodded. "Mayfield did a lot of talking for about a month there. Stuff about traffic flow, re-engagement of underutilized civic assets, that kind of thing."

"What is that supposed to mean?" I asked.

Trixie shrugged. "I wasn't all that clear on it either," she said, "but I was going a little cross-eyed by that point. He seems to have made his case, every paper in town ran an editorial in support of the new plan."

I raised an eyebrow. "There is nothing quite so suspicious as a room full of newshawks agreeing on anything."

Trixie made a face. "It might not be as exciting as all that," she said. "Bringing the expressway into the city means tearing down a fair piece of the place where it lands. It might just be cheaper to run it through Riverton. There's not much there."

"Is that what 'underutilized civic asset' means?" I asked. "Too poor to object?"

"Too poor for anybody to give a damn anyway," Trixie said. "But it's mostly federal money, so I don't know why City Hall is counting the beans. I can't see any way for them to put the leftovers into their own pockets. But one way or another, your mousey little City Planner is in charge of millions of dollars and the destiny of untold masses."

I smiled. "Well, Glory Be," I said. "This is why he rates a cover-up."

Trixie nodded. "He's at the front of the pack right now, which means if he gets publicly humiliated, it smears the whole job. There are plenty of pictures of Mayfield speaking at public meetings with the Mayor or a Councilman or two in the shot. He might be a lot more important than he thinks he is."

"Okay," I said, "so what does all that have to do with his dead mistress, her dead ex-boyfriend with the dirty pictures or the entire Rossetti crime family?"

Trixie shrugged. "I dunno, let's go ask him."

"Ask who?" I said, a little lost.

"Roger Mayfield," she said simply.

"Isn't that what I wanted to do at nine o'clock in the morning?" I asked, annoyed.

"Nine thirty-seven," she reminded. "And there's a difference."

"Which is?" I asked.

"When you wanted to do it, it was a stupid idea," she said with a smile.

"Ah," I said, "of course."

"You ready for one of those hot dogs yet?" she asked.

I thought about it and decided that I was.

Chapter Eighteen

Jack tried telephoning Roger Mayfield first, which I told him was a waste of time. But he argued that Mayfield was still his employer and was the closest thing that either of us had to a reason to pursue this case beyond the motivated self-interest of not wanting to be stuck in the middle of an open murder investigation and a general desire not to look like a pair of public jackasses. It was an interesting point.

Interesting, but futile. When he called from the drugstore, Jack was told that Mister Mayfield was in a meeting and would he please try again later? By the time we got to the payphones in the lobby at City Hall, Mister Mayfield was out of the office and would be for the rest of the day. Jack said the response was frosty, rapid-fire and came the moment that he had said his name. Word had clearly gone out that Jack Justice was persona non grata, which sounded about right.

We checked the directory for the City Planner's office and headed up in the elevator to fourth. The hope was that by moving quickly, the girl at the desk would never associate the visitors with the man who called a moment ago. I hoped this argument held because the building was full of cops, and Miss Dixon had seen about enough of them lately.

I took the lead when we walked in the office. There was a central reception desk and a small maze of office doors beyond. Mayfield didn't even have his own secretary, how important could this guy be?

I smiled my polite but not dazzling smile. There was no need to dazzle the help; indeed it would only attract the wrong kind of attention.

"Can I help you?" the woman asked me with a tight, forced civil-service smile.

"I wonder if I could speak to Roger Mayfield, please," I asked.

She eyed me suspiciously for a moment. "Do you have an appointment?" she asked.

"No, I'm sorry, I just popped in, is that terrible?" I smiled again. "His wife Anne and I went to school together, and I just wanted to say hello."

"And your name?" she asked, lifting the receiver. Brisk, but polite.

"Timms," I said. "Janet Timms."

Roger Mayfield came out ten seconds later at a trot with his eyes spinning in counter-clockwise circles. He looked at me without comprehension and Jack saved him before he could say something stupid.

"Mister Mayfield," he said with his best brush salesman's manner. "Ray Green, we spoke on the phone. Janet said she was going to stop in and I thought I'd come with, you don't mind, do you?"

Mayfield was ashen-faced, but he kept it together.

"No, that's fine," he said. "It's nice to see you both. I only have a few minutes…"

"Of course," I said, turning the smile up several degrees, mostly for the benefit of the girl at the desk. "I'd love to see your office, though."

That seemed to move things along. Mayfield was still in a malleable state, but that wasn't going to last for very long. He led us down a hallway and into a door that was farther apart than most of the others, which I took to mean it was a little bigger. The room looked comfortable and neat. Too put-together for a guy like this to have done himself. I wondered if Anne Mayfield had done it up for him or if that was handled by the woman at the desk. She didn't look like the office squeeze type, but Mayfield didn't look much like a Lothario, so maybe you can't always tell.

The door closed behind us.

"What are you playing at?" Mayfield hissed at Jack, his voice low, suggesting that the walls were not exactly sound-proof.

"You wouldn't take my calls, sir," Jack said simply.

"I am trying to keep things quiet and not attract attention," Mayfield said.

"No," Jack said with a shake of his head. "If you were doing that you'd have taken my call and talked to me quietly. What you were doing was ducking me, and that attracts more attention. You told the girl at the desk that you were not in for any calls from a Jack Justice, didn't you? How often do you do things like that?"

"Hardly ever," he admitted quietly.

"Hardly ever," Jack nodded. "You're in the middle of something pretty terrible, sir, and I'm sorry for that. But you're under the impression that if you pretend everything is normal, it will be. And I don't see it playing out that way."

"This is being handled," he said. "Janet's death isn't even in the papers."

Jack and I exchanged a look. "Yes, sir, we noticed that. But just because the police are playing with kid gloves today doesn't mean you're in the clear."

"I spoke to the police, I told them everything," Mayfield said, drawing himself up to his full height.

Jack nodded. "I hope so, sir," he said. "It'll make it easier to remember when you tell it to me."

Mayfield bristled. "Why should I?" he asked.

"Because you're my client," Jack said, "and I can't act on your behalf if I don't know what you want. If you keep me in the dark, I'm likely to blunder into something you'd rather I kept out of, and none of us want that, sir."

Mayfield thought about that. He didn't agree, but he thought about it, and that was something.

"Does the name Jimmy Lish mean anything to you?" Jack asked.

Mayfield blinked. "Lish?" he said. "He went with Janet for a while. A photographer, I think."

"Sort of," Jack nodded. "Also a blackmailer."

Mayfield swallowed hard. "Lish?" he said weakly. "What are you doing, snooping around Jimmy Lish anyway?"

"You told me to, sir," Jack's words were conciliatory, but his voice was as cold and grey as stone. "You hired me to find your blackmailer."

"Lish?" Mayfield said again. "How did he know about Janet and me? I never even met the man."

"I don't know, sir," Jack said, "but it seems likely that he found out from Miss Timms."

Roger Mayfield set his jaw hard and blinked back tears that seemed to come quite suddenly. "No, Mister Justice. Janet would never do that. She hated Lish, hated him for… things he made her do."

"She told you about that?" Jack asked.

Mayfield started like he had been slapped. This was getting to be too much for him. He was holding his act together with both hands, but it wasn't going to keep.

"You talked to Lish?" Mayfield asked.

"Lish is dead," Jack said simply.

Roger Mayfield wobbled on his feet and turned ashen. I thought that he might faint.

"Lish?" he asked. "Dead?"

"Yes, sir," Jack said grimly. "Somebody tossed his place and shot him dead. Tried to burn it too, but didn't make a proper job of it. The cops'll be days sorting through Lish's files, but it looks like if there was anything there that proved a link to Miss Timms or yourself, it was taken."

"Taken?" Mayfield still seemed startled.

"Yes, sir," Jack said, "by someone who knew what they were looking for."

Roger Mayfield stood quietly for a moment, lost in thought.

"Then there isn't any proof that it was Lish who sent me the picture," he said. "You don't know that it was him."

"No, sir," Jack said. "But the police know that you suspected blackmail, and they know that your girlfriend is dead and her blackmailer ex-boyfriend is too. And they may not think much of me, but they know that I didn't do it. So even if they had actually crossed you off their list of suspects, which I doubt, you're back on it now. We just have a few more questions, sir."

Mayfield stared into the middle distance. Jack looked at me.

"I wondered what you could tell us about the Long Branch Expressway, sir," I said. "Specifically the decision to re-route it through the Riverton area."

Mayfield stared at me as if he had just noticed me for the first time. "What?" he said blankly.

"The Riverton route, sir," I repeated. "It seems a little counterintuitive. I wondered if you can tell us where the idea had its genesis."

"Who are you?" Mayfield said, suddenly horrified.

"My associate, Miss Dixon," Jack said simply.

"Trixie, please," I said.

"The... the other desk?" Mayfield said slowly filling in the gaps for himself and constructing a much more believable story in the process. "The second desk in your office... you didn't mention..."

"No, sir," Jack said. "What can you tell us about the new route?"

"It... it isn't new," Mayfield said. "It was a possibility from the earliest feasibility reports."

"Yes, sir," I said, "but now it's the top dog. Can you tell us how that happened?'

Mayfield blinked several times. He looked like he was prepared to bolt from the room. "What on Earth does this have to do with Janet and I?"

I shook my head. "We don't know, sir," I said. "But there has been some pretty serious influence wielded on your behalf in the last couple of days, keeping this out of the papers and all."

Mayfield looked from me to Jack and back again.

"It seemed to us that the only thing you do that's big enough to merit that kind of attention is the Long Branch Project," I continued, "and the biggest news in the Long Branch Project is the Riverton route."

"If there are interested players that powerful," Jack explained, "you might be in some danger and not know it."

"Danger?" Mayfield almost broke out laughing, but his eyes were full of panic. "The only danger I'm in is the fool of a private detective I hired blowing this…" His voice trailed off and he looked at me with new consideration. "You said your name was… Dixon?"

I nodded. We were blown and there was no point trying to cover it now.

Mayfield looked at Jack. "The policeman said that you were shooting at another private detective when Janet died. Named Dixon."

Jack said nothing.

"Why would you be shooting at your own partner?" Mayfield blinked.

"How much time do you have?" Jack said with a shrug.

Mayfield whipped his head around to me. "Who are you working for?" he snapped.

"Now?" I said. "Nobody."

"And when Janet was murdered?"

"Another interested party," I said.

"Get out of here," Mayfield said in a voice that must have carried to the next office in spite of his care. "Get out of here and don't come back, you hear me? You're off the case. Finished."

We stepped out into the hall and he closed the door behind us as quickly as he could.

"Think he's calling his playmates?" I asked.

Jack shook his head. "Building security first," he said. "Let's get out of here."

"He knows who's pulling the strings around here," I said as we walked down the hall, interested onlookers peeping out of their offices like timid doormice. "Did you hear him say this was 'being handled'?"

"I heard him," Jack said.

"He knows," I said.

"He knows something," Jack said. "He doesn't know who killed his girlfriend, but he has a general idea of who's going to kill him if he doesn't get a lid on this, and fast."

We left the City Planner's office and headed for the fire stairs rather than meet our escort at the elevator. I pushed the door open with my hip and paused a moment, considering something.

"We're dead, aren't we?" I asked without emotion.

"Yeah," Jack said. "Very."

We walked down the stairs quickly, but in silence.

"I guess that's a good reason to see this through," I said at last.

"It isn't a good reason," said Jack, "but it's a reason. And it isn't like we were going to stop anyway."

Chapter Nineteen

I pointed the car toward Riverton. I don't really know why, except we had been talking about the place for most of the day and it occurred to me I hadn't been there for years. Nobody went to Riverton. It wasn't exactly a slum. Most of the places in the city that qualified for that name were pretty strongly weighted with one ethnic population or another. They were poor places, to be sure, and outsiders were often afraid of them, but they could also be vibrant and full of life. I grant you, that was taking sort of a *National Geographic* approach, and I'm sure that people in places like Meadowview and Topside might take odds with the idea. But there were people there. Riverton was just kind of empty.

I had no trouble finding a place to park, that much was certain. When we stepped out onto the streets, mine was the only car in sight.

"Cozy," I said.

"I don't remember it being like this," Trixie said, "but it's been a while."

"Yeah," I said.

"So what are we doing here?" she asked.

"I don't know," I said, looking around at all of the nothing.

"Oh good," she said, "at least there's a plan."

"You got your notes with you?" I asked.

"Sure," she said warily.

"Bring 'em," I said. "Let's walk the route."

"What's the point?" she asked.

"No idea," I said with a shrug. "Let's find out."

She looked at me like she was wishing me a large, fatal bowel obstruction, but she took her notepad out of her handbag and flipped them open.

"The Long Branch will run along the river to Basin," she said, "and then come up through Magee and Jefferson."

I frowned and looked at her. Those streets ran parallel. "Which is it?" I asked. "Magee or Jefferson?"

"Both," she said. "The block between them. All the way up to Austin Road."

I whistled. She nodded.

"This is a massive thing, Jack," she said, "a ton of people in and out, every morning, every night."

I nodded. "I can see why they're looking at Riverton," I said. "Imagine how much it would cost to tear up St. Ives or Lincoln to take this right downtown."

Trixie frowned. "But taking them right downtown is the point," she said. "Nobody works in Riverton."

"Maybe now they will," I said, walking towards Magee Street. "Come on."

"You really think so?" she asked me, and I could tell that she didn't care what I thought, she wanted to tell me what she did. I gave her a look that said both that I knew what she was after and was a grudging invitation to continue. Amazingly, she seemed to get both messages at once, which was a pretty tall order for somebody I had known for two days.

"If you ask me," she said, "this whole expressway business is nuts."

I snorted by way of reply.

"No, I mean it," she said. "I get why a guy who lives in the suburbs wants one, sure. His job is in the city and his life is somewhere else. And I get why the Feds want to throw money at it, 'cause the folks with all the money are the ones moving out of the city. "

"Not the big money," I said.

"No, maybe not the big money," she said, "but those guys have always had houses in three places."

I nodded. "Granted."

"But why is City Hall buying into this?" she asked. "You really think that if you tear down half of Riverton and fill it with cars, that anybody's gonna get out of their cars when they're here? Right before they get on the magic carpet back to the sticks, they're gonna stop and do a little shopping?"

I shrugged. "Could happen," I said.

"But it won't," she said.

"Nope," I agreed.

"So all you've really done is made things easier for the guy that doesn't live here," she said. "And maybe because it's so easy to get in and out, maybe more people leave. And maybe the only people left are the ones too poor to get out."

"Well," I said, shoving my hands in my coat pockets, "we shall live as kings among lesser men."

"I'm serious," she said.

"Let me get this straight," I said. "There's, what, hundreds of millions of dollars being spent all over the country on these things? In just about every city you can name. And everybody says it'll bring prosperity for generations to come. But you know better."

"That's right," she said without irony.

"We like ourselves, don't we?" I asked.

She shrugged. "Gotta like somebody," she said, "and the only other person around is you, so obviously that isn't an option."

"Obviously," I said, and stopped dead.

"What's wrong?" she asked.

"You said it's the block between Magee and Jefferson?" I asked.

"So?"

"So look at it," I said.

She did, and whistled in a low tone. I nodded without looking at her, and we walked like two gunslingers into an old west ghost town. There was nothing. I didn't think Riverton could get more deserted, but here it was. Almost every building was shuttered or boarded up. Those few that weren't had fallen into serious disrepair, and only a handful of lights were on in the windows above in spite of the deepening shadows. We walked in silence over to Jefferson. It was all the same.

"Which way?" she asked. "Down or up?"

I looked down. Basin Street. There hadn't been much there fifteen years ago, when this was still a real neighborhood. "Up," I said, and we walked.

We saw no one on the sidewalks. A few cars went by but they moved quickly, as though they had no intention of stopping until they were far from here.

"When did the city start buying up these buildings again?" I asked.

She shook her head and looked at her notes. "It hasn't," she said. "The final vote on the new route isn't for three weeks. Then the appropriations committee is formed."

"Wow," I said. "This block has had some bad luck."

"For a while, by the look of it," Trixie said. "Some of these places look like they've been shut for years."

"Okay, but why?" I asked. "I know it's a lousy neighborhood, I get it. But why are there shops and apartments and…."

"Things?" she offered helpfully.

"Sure," I said, "things. There are things a block to the east, and things a block to the west. And in the middle there is a big pile of nothing."

"Yes," she said.

"And it is through this big pile of nothing that they wish to put an expressway costing millions of dollars."

"Yes," she agreed.

"That seems convenient," I said.

"It does, doesn't it?" she nodded.

"Mayfield said the Riverton Route was always part of the plan, didn't he?" I asked.

"He said it was in the earliest feasibility reports," she said. "But it was a backup plan."

"How old are those reports?" I asked.

She frowned. "I don't think I have that," she said, flipping through her notebook. "Before the war anyway. The whole thing got put on hold for a while there."

"Yeah," I said, "a lot of things did."

She looked around. The girl detective did not rattle easily, but I could tell this place was giving her the creeps. Me too.

"So what are you thinking?" she asked. "You think somebody bought up Riverton just in case they decided to run an expressway through it?"

"Maybe," I said.

"And then let it all go to hell, because they were just waiting to sell it to the government?" Her tone seemed increasingly dubious.

"Maybe," I said.

"That'd be a hell of a risk," she said. "They only started talking about changing the route a few months ago."

"Yeah," I said.

"And these expropriations," she said, getting frustrated with my terse replies, "they aren't gonna be like winning the lottery. I mean, these landlords will do all right, better than the state of the place deserves, but it wouldn't be that much of a high percentage payout if you bought the place just to sell it like that."

"It's true," I agreed.

"So who would pull a stunt like that?" she asked.

"I don't know," I said. "Maybe somebody who has loads of untraceable liquid cash, and a long-term goal of legitimizing the family business."

"Rossetti," she hissed.

"He sells all of this to the government and he cleans every dollar he put into it," I said. "At a stroke, he's legit."

"Stella mentioned that he'd been buying up buildings for years," Trixie nodded.

I made an expansive shrug with my hands wide apart.

"Means he's been working on this for a long time," she said.

"And perhaps explains why the stunning Janet Timms wound up with the much less stunning Roger Mayfield," I said.

"Holy cats," she said.

"Yeah."

"We are so very dead," she said.

"Yeah."

Trixie looked around. "Well," she said, "the ownership of these building is a matter of public record. He's probably got them owned by dummy companies, but I bet we can tie them to him if we get the time."

I shook my head. "He'd never leave us walking around that long if we started digging. Right now, he might wait to see what we do. I don't exactly have a squeaky-clean reputation, and that's by design. Mayfield fired me, you're off the case. Rossetti might wait to see what we do."

"Would you?" she asked.

I shrugged. "It isn't exactly illegal to buy up buildings," I said, "or to profit from government contracts. The news that Rossetti owns this neighborhood might queer the vote, and it might not. He's greased a lot of palms downtown and I'm not sure the electorate would really give a damn."

"And we don't have much more than a handful of mumbles about anything else," Trixie said. "So what do we do? You don't want to find out for sure who owns these buildings?"

I spotted a small, squat building ahead with a neon sign lit up in the window. "Sure I do," I said, "but let's try and do it another way."

Chapter Twenty

The sign in the window said, "Spenser's Place". Its construction probably made more sense to the casual observer when the buildings on either side of it were still standing. Right now it looked like it had been air-dropped into the middle of a quiet desolation, as though having delivered peace and democracy, the U.S. Air Force was now sending the world third-rate gin-holes.

I stepped through the door and was hit by a wall of stale air delicately scented by stale beer. The low light didn't do much to hide the cobwebs in the high corners, but only because I was looking for them. Whatever else he might be, Mister Spenser was not much of a housekeeper. The place could do with what they used to call a "woman's touch", when what they really meant was "a couple of hours of back-breaking labor". It seemed unlikely to get it, to judge by the astonished faces turned towards me from the bar. There were six barflies in the place, all seated around the long bar, none of them seated next to one another. It looked like the sort of place where you stared quietly into your beer for a few hours wondering where it all went wrong. They had all turned when the door opened, and stayed turned when they saw yours truly. Apparently it was ladies night, for the first and only time ever. Hooray.

"Evening, folks," said a gruff but booming voice from behind the bar. "Can I help you find something?"

"You can help us find a couple of beers," Jack said, sidling up to an open space at the bar. I joined him, not out of any desire to do so, but from the logical standpoint that standing apart from my gentleman companion might be seen as an invitation for one or more of the moping barflies to try his luck. That was a conversation devoutly to be missed, so I stuck with Jack.

The bartender pulled his tap open, and began filling a glass. "What brings you folks down here?" he asked.

Jack shrugged. "Nostalgia, I guess," he said. "I used to have a place down here years ago, before the war."

The bartender nodded. His neck was thick and his hands were like two large, flattened out hams. His nose had the look like it had been broken once and not set quite right, but some guys just kind of looked like that when they hit sixty, and if this guy was a day younger, I'd eat my best sleuthing hat.

"Whereabouts?" he asked, putting the glass down in front of me and staring on a second.

"Down Jefferson," Jack said. "Apartment above that old fix-it shop, what was it called, Donald's?"

I hadn't seen a sign for a Donald's Fix-It Shop out on the streets. Maybe Jack was on the level.

The bartender smiled and nodded. "Donald Morse," he said, "now there was a funny duck." One of the barflies laughed a little, just for half an instant, as if remembering something that was not exactly funny but was funnier than the nothing he'd been thinking of for the last hour. "He's been gone almost ten years now," the bartender said, still smiling a little. "Heart attack, I think."

The barflies nodded and mostly went back to their beers. The second beer was set down.

"You've been here a long time, then," Jack said. "Funny, I don't remember this place."

"Nah," the man said with a grin. "This was my beat. Twenty-six years. I opened this place when I retired from the force."

"Ex-copper, huh?" Jack smiled. "I could tell by the neck."

The man smiled. "My youngest daughter got married three years back, I had a devil of a time finding a collar that would close around it." He held out a meaty paw toward Jack. "Hap Spenser," he said.

"Nice to meet you, Hap," Jack said, shaking the man's hand. "I'm Jack and this is Trixie."

"Trixie, is it?" Hap said with a smile. "And what is a flower such as yourself doing with a man who brings you down to a place such as this?"

I nodded. "It is an interesting question," I said.

"We were just in the neighborhood," Jack said.

"For what, I can't imagine," Hap said, wiping down his side of the bar with a rag as though he did it all the time, which casual observation suggested that he did not.

"Like I say, just playing the memory game," Jack said, taking a pull on his beer. I did the same, it wasn't bad. Jack pointed to a picture behind the bar. "Is that Roxy?" he asked.

· I looked up. The picture was of a younger Hap Spenser, in uniform, with a large, expansive woman of about forty-five. Hap smiled. "It is," he said. "That one used to hang in her Deli. She gave it to me when she shut down her place, maybe six years ago."

"No Roxy's?" Jack seemed astonished.

Hap shook his head sadly. "No Roxy's." He looked at me, finding someone he could tell the happier part of the story to. "Roxy's Deli used to be the busiest place in twenty blocks. All day and night they would be in there, and once you had been in once, you understood why."

Jack joined in. "The place had a real balanced diet. Meat and bread. Not a vegetable in sight."

"Coleslaw is a vegetable," Hap protested.

"Holy crow, I forgot about the coleslaw," Jack said with a shake of his head. He looked back to the picture. "She was quite a lady."

Hap nodded. "Just about ran the neighborhood," he said, "back when there was one. She held on longer than she should have. Spent most of what she'd saved trying to hold on, hoping things would come back. But they never did."

They talked a little more about a delicatessen that I had never been to and now never would. I looked around the

*small, dank room and realized that it was full of pictures
like that. Not the usual photos and clippings of half-
forgotten boxers and ballplayers, but all ordinary people
in ordinary places, mostly with a beaming Hap Spenser
standing there in uniform. The place was a shrine to a
Riverton that was gone. Gone but not forgotten, not yet.*

"So what happened?" I asked.

Hap Spenser frowned. "What's that, my dear?"

*"To the whole place," I said as much as possible as
though I had never been there in my life. "Why is
everything shut, shuttered or torn right down?"*

*Hap nodded. He would rather not talk about it, but was
too much of a gentleman not to respond to a lady's
question. "Funny story that. They tore down the building
to the north because it was condemned. Falling apart on
its feet, it was. It was falling apart because it had been
standing empty for years, no one paying the smallest
attention to it. But finally it was too much, and they took a
wrecking ball to it. The vibrations from the wreck were too
much for the place to the south, and it half fell apart while
they were working, so the city tore it down too."*

*I took a sip of my beer. "But it isn't just that," I said.
"This whole block looks condemned, except for this place.
Everything's empty the whole way up."*

*Some of the barflies shifted uncomfortably. Maybe they
didn't want to see Hap get riled up. Maybe this is where
they came to forget what had happened to their
neighborhood.*

*Hap smiled and had a faraway look in his eye. "It
happened so gradually, little girl, I never even noticed it.
Riverton was never a rich place, it wasn't that unusual for
a building to stand empty for a time now and then. But
then they would sell and nothing would ever happen to
them. Or an apartment building would sell and be left to
rot. Just slowly fell apart over time until almost everyone
was gone. All the way up to Austin. And when you cut a*

neighborhood in half like that, soon everything on either side starts to rot away, like a hollow log. The folks that were here started leaving, and no one came in to take their place." He looked at Jack. "You were lucky that you got out when you did," he said.

Jack shook his head. "I wasn't here long. I bounced around a lot in those days."

"Sure," Hap nodded. "Lots of folks did."

"Not you though," Jack said, nodding at the pictures that lined the room.

Hap smiled a little at the faces on the walls, most of them impossible to make out in the semi-darkness, but he knew who they were. "No," he said, "not me. I just kind of fell in love with the place. You understand, this was back when being a neighborhood cop meant something. The department didn't move you around the way they do today. These kids these days, as soon as they're in a uniform, they're looking to get out of it, make detective or some nonsense, like there's no pride in being a cop. Some of them never seem to get out of their prowl cars. They just drive around."

Jack nodded. "I guess they reckon the radio cars are more efficient."

Hap snorted at the word. "Those boys are missing something special, sitting in those cars," he said. "They'll never know a place the way that I knew Riverton. And they'll never be that place's protector the way that I was."

Jack set down his beer. "Not much left to protect."

"No," came the quiet reply.

"Roxy hung on too long, you say."

Hap's brows furrowed. "She did."

"So what about you?" Jack asked.

Several barflies got up from their stools and moved the hell away from us.

"Oh good," I said quietly to no one in particular.

"You ever think about selling out?"

Hap Spenser reached below the bar and came up with a shotgun. It was such a smooth motion that I never saw it coming. He took a step back behind the bar and leveled it at Black Jack. Jack didn't move.

"I know who sent you," Spenser said.

"Who sent me?" Jack asked quietly.

"You're one of his boys," Spenser said. "You're one of Rossetti's mob."

Jack took a pull on his beer. May as well play it casual. If that pop-gun was even loaded with bird-shot it would tear his face off at this range. "Do I look like a soldier in the Rossetti family?" he asked.

Hap Spenser's aim was steady. "Maybe not," he said. "Maybe because I said I'd put the next one in the ground."

"Maybe," Jack said.

"Rossetti's tried to buy you out?" I asked.

Spenser did not look at me. If I thought he might have pulled the trigger, I could have dropped him easy. But he was a cop. A real cop. He reeked of it. He was no murderer. "You seem like a real nice girl," Spenser said, "but you have some bad friends. Al Rossetti killed Riverton. Killed it as sure as if he'd pulled the trigger on every man, woman and child that used to call this place home. I know that he owns half these empty buildings, and he probably owns the other half too."

"Can you prove it?" Jack said, staring down the barrel of the shotgun.

"No, I can't prove it," Hap spat, "and even if I could, it ain't against the law. It ought to be, but it isn't. But he's a murdering scum, a gangster. And I'll be damned if he's going to get my place."

Jack nodded and set his glass on the bar, quietly. "He's tried before?"

Spenser snorted. "Don't play dumb," he said.

"I am dumb," Jack said. "Ask anyone. Ask her."

"It's true," I said.

"Rossetti's sent his smooth boys and he's sent his rough boys," Spenser said. "The first ones got a polite 'go to hell', the rest got better than that. The last ones I put in the hospital, I told them the next ones I'll put in the morgue. Maybe they didn't get my message."

"I don't work for Rossetti," Jack said.

"Then who do you work for?" Spenser said.

"Myself," Jack said. "I'm a private detective."

"A private...," Hap Spenser had a look of genuine disgust on his face. "You expect me to believe that?"

"Doesn't matter what you believe," Jack said. "Fact is if we wished you harm, you would be dead now."

"And how would you do that, smart-guy?" Spenser asked.

"Ask her," Jack said, barely moving his eyes toward me.

Spenser made the smallest motion of his eyes, and could not help but notice that I now had the Beretta on him.

"Hello," I said.

"Jesus Christ," came the reply.

"Put it down," I said. "Nice and slow."

He did it. He didn't like it, but he did it all right.

"So now Rossetti's sending women after me," he said.

"We don't work for Rossetti," I said, flipping a business card onto the bar. Spenser looked at it but did not move.

Jack reached into his pocket for change to pay for the drinks.

"I don't want your money," Spenser said.

"You can throw it out after we leave, then," Jack said, putting it on the bar.

"One of the barflies is on the payphone," I said.

"Cops?" Jack asked.

"Or Rossetti, I guess," I said. "Either way, I'd quite like to be somewhere else."

Jack nodded and stood. "That sounds about right," he said. He looked at the thick-necked ex-bull behind the bar, standing with his hands raised slightly.

"I wish I could help you," Jack said. "But I'm not sure that anybody can.

Chapter Twenty-One

We walked back to my car in silence. The world failed entirely to collapse on us as we made our retreat. We discovered no corpses, not even a little one. We were neither arrested nor detained, in fact the only police car we saw was heading quickly in the opposite direction, though in all fairness, it may have finally been responding to a small disturbance we had at least helped to cause back at Hap Spenser's bar. By the time I unlocked the doors of the heap and we piled in, the evening seemed to have lost a little steam. I started the engine and pulled away from the curb.

The city sky was as black as it ever seemed to get, and the lights of the passing shops blinked through the windows as we drove. Trixie shifted uncomfortably in her seat. I wondered if she was working up to some revelation, or if the little hidden piece she wore was chafing her.

"Well," she said at last.

I waited a moment to see if there was more. There did not seem to be.

"Yeah," I agreed.

"Yeah," she said.

We drove in silence for another minute.

"This was fun and all," she said at last, "but I'm not sure it's going anywhere."

There didn't seem to be anything to say to that, so I didn't.

"Well?" she asked a moment later, proving that I had once again misread the situation. I hadn't worked with anyone since old Tom packed it in after the war, and he and I had never talked all that much. Maybe that was because we had worked together for so many years. Maybe it was just because neither of us was a leggy blonde, or any other sort of girl detective.

"Well what?" I shrugged.

"You don't have any opinion on that?" she asked.

I thought about it for a minute. "I'm not sure I remember what the question was," I said.

"You really are the original horse's ass, aren't you?" she asked.

I grinned. "It took you this long to notice?" I asked.

"In my defense," she said, "I did try to kill you right after we met."

"If that was trying to kill me," I said, "you're a lousy shot."

"Oh clam up, jackass," she said. "A .22 isn't for serious work."

"No, it isn't," I said.

"Where are we going?" she asked.

"I'm driving you home," I said.

"How do you know where I live?" she asked, mildly horrified.

"You aren't serious," I said. "Gosh, it's almost like there was some sort of published directory of addresses and telephone numbers."

"Okay, shut up," she said.

"How many Trixie Dixons do you think there are, anyway?" I asked.

"I said shut up," she said.

"If you hadn't showed up at my office, I did have a Plan B, you know."

This statement got a little more attention than I had intended it to.

"Really," she asked, "and what would that have been?"

"I just mean that I knew where you could be found," I said, "in office hours and otherwise. Keep in mind, I'd been hired to find a blackmailer, and I thought that it was you."

"Well, that was a pretty stupid thing to think," she snorted.

"Yeah, you're right," I said. "Girl setting up a camera from the same window from which certain candid shots of my client and his mistress had been taken, couldn't be who I was looking for at all."

We drove in silence for another minute.

"She had to be in on it," Trixie muttered.

"In on what?" I asked. "The blackmail?"

"Sure, the blackmail," Trixie said. "A girl who looks like that is used to having eyes on her every moment of every day. No way she forgets to close those blinds."

"Heat of passion?" I asked.

"For Roger Mayfield?" she asked with both eyebrows arched at once, which I didn't even know was possible.

"Yeah, see, this is what I thought," I said, turning left on to Grange.

"But if Janet Timms was playing cozy with Roger Mayfield because Rossetti asked her to, or told her to, why would she get Jimmy Lish involved?" she protested. "Why take that kind of risk?"

"Maybe Lish didn't exactly ask," I said. "Maybe he just told. Maybe Janet Timms had a little trouble saying 'no' to a man who used to have a hold over her."

"Maybe he still did have a hold over her," Trixie said.

"Lish's files? Think he had a couple of hundred pictures she'd rather the world didn't see?" It wasn't a bad thought. "I guess we'll never know now."

"Yeah," she agreed.

There was another moment of silence.

"But still, what would make Mayfield a target for blackmail?" Trixie said with a shake of her head. "He's important, if you care where the expressway goes. If you don't, he's nothing."

"Was there any money?" I asked.

She shook her head. "It was all the wife's."

Neither one of us had anything to say about that for a minute. The traffic coming off Clinton was heavy for this time of night.

"Maybe she didn't know that," I offered. "Maybe all she knew is that Big Al asked her to spend some time keeping Mayfield happy. She didn't know what he'd done to deserve it, but figured there must be some action there somewhere, so she calls Lish and tries to cut herself a piece."

Trixie scowled. "My big problem with that is that it casts her as the villain who deserved what she got," she said. "How about Rossetti forced her to sleep with Mayfield and Lish forced her to let him document the occasion. And then somebody killed her for being in the middle. How about that?"

I nodded. "It still sings," I said. "Though my big problem with that is that it casts her as the helpless victim. A plaything and pawn in a world of cunning and guileful men."

Trixie nodded. "It kind of does, doesn't it?"

"The truth is probably somewhere in the vastness between the two," I said.

"So what now?" she asked.

I thought about it for a minute.

"I'm not sure that this is going anywhere," I said.

"You jackass," she hissed. "I said that five minutes ago."

"I know," I said. "I was agreeing with you."

"Oh," she said.

"I mean, there's pretty clearly something shifty going on in Riverton," I said, "but I'm not sure it's illegal."

"It probably is if there's a proven link between Mayfield and Rossetti," Trixie said.

"Yeah, probably," I agreed. "Bearing in mind that's not the kind of detective work that we're very good at-"

"You mean there's a kind that you are very good at?" she asked. "Were you planning on ever doing some of it?"

"Shut up," I said. "That's not detecting, that's accounting. The cops and the D.A., they have guys for that, they have ever since they got Capone for tax evasion."

"You aren't going to wax all nostalgic for the good old days, are you, Flat-Top? Speakeasies and such?"

"I keep saying shut up," I said, "and you keep not shutting up at all."

"I'm funny that way," she said.

"My point is, that's not what we do," I said. "We can't subpoena bank records and things like that, and I doubt very much we'd find anyone downtown willing to try."

"Which you are basing on...?"

"The fact that there are forces up high that just got Sabien to kill a story that might have put me out of business," I said. "They must have laid it on pretty thick if they put a scare in that big boy."

Trixie nodded. "See, this is kind of my point," she said.

"What is?" I picked up the thread. "The fact that the dogs are unlikely to be called off in the next few weeks, what with the Federal money set to flow and the final vote on the route coming up? City Hall will keep the pressure up, and Rossetti will keep the pressure up, and that means that Mike Rogers will never get to write our little Mutt and Jeff story."

"I hate it when people finish my thoughts," she said. "Especially when I don't like them very much."

I nodded. "That must be very annoying," I agreed. "But I'm right, yes?"

"Yes," she said. "And not to be practical about this, but neither of us is exactly employed right now. And we're not gonna stumble over a fee in the middle of this mess."

"True," I said. "And if somebody offered me a straight fee to get in the middle of a business deal that Al Rossetti had been setting up for years, I'm not sure they make a retainer big enough for that one."

"Yeah," she agreed.

We drove another six blocks in silence.

"I feel bad about Janet Timms," she said. "I feel like we're abandoning her."

"I never met her," I said. "I saw a photograph that she'd have rather I didn't, and I saw her cross the street one time."

"So you don't feel bad?" she asked.

"Sure I do," I said.

"Good," Trixie said with a smile. "I'd hate to think I was the only sucker in town."

I laughed. "What about Jimmy Lish?" I asked.

"He was a blackmailer and a pornographer," she said.

"Does that mean that he deserved it?" I asked.

"I don't know," she shrugged. "But it means he didn't have the right to be real surprised. And it means that I don't give much of a damn."

"Do you think that some people deserve it?" I asked.

"Yes," she said after a moment. "Do you?"

"Yes," I said. "But that's not really my job. Not anymore."

She didn't say anything to that, and I was glad.

"Worst case scenario?" she asked.

I shrugged. "I can tip off Mike Rogers that we have a swell line if the story ever does break," I said. "I won't tell him anything unless I get the word, then he'll have gangsters, politicians, civil servants, pornographers and fallen women to write about. To say nothing of millions of taxpayer dollars going into the pockets of one of the most notorious criminals in the city. There won't be any room for you or me in that story."

She nodded. "So that's it, then," she said.

I nodded. "I guess so," I said.

We drove another minute in silence. I turned right onto Oakwood and stopped in front of her building.

"Well," she said, "it made for an interesting change from divorce work."

I nodded. "I'll bet it did," I said.

"Well, Black Jack, this was fun," she said opening the door. "Let's not do it again, okay?"

And then she was gone.

Chapter Twenty-Two

The pounding at the door jarred me awake. It had taken on the rhythmic tempo of knocking that had been going on for a long time, and my first impulse was to shoot somebody. To be completely accurate, my first impulse was to shoot Jack, since I was sure it was him. The knocking was irritating and random, which in a short time I had clearly come to associate with Black Jack Justice. As I fumbled for the Beretta on the nightstand, my eyes focused on the clock. Six in the morning. Couldn't be Jack. Too late to be up late, too Jack to be up early.

I stepped out of the bedroom into the sitting room. "Just a minute," I called, mostly to make the knocking stop, though I had given away any element of surprise I might have held in the process. The things we do to keep our neighbors from complaining.

The room was mostly dark and I kept it that way. The light spill from the lamp in the hall might give my position away. I crept closer to the doorway and gripped the Beretta hard. It occurred to me at last that this could be a visitor from our friend Big Al Rossetti, who might not have gotten the news just yet that we had given up snooping in his backyard. I slid close to the peephole and spotted the cop on the other side. I set the Beretta down on a shelf behind the door and turned the knob, opening the door as far as the safety chain would allow.

"What is it?" I said.

"Police, Miss," the uniform stammered.

It occurred to me for the first time that I had reached for my handgun as a normal girl might reach for her robe and in the process had not covered up my sleeping attire, which was soft and satiny and clung to my curves. Even at six a.m., Miss Dixon could distract the forces of law and order. Good to know.

"I know who you are, Peaches," I said. "What I want to know is why you're beating an irregular bosa nova on my poor little door at this ungodly hour."

"Lieutenant Sabien, Miss," the poor kid stumbled, "he wants you. That is, he wants you downtown. I mean he told me to bring you there. Downtown, I mean."

"You really need to work on your entrance," I said. "If you like I could close the door and we could try it again."

"No, thank you, Miss," he said, furrowing his eyebrows and trying to look stern and unaroused.

"Tell Lieutenant Sabien that I'll pencil him in for ten-thirty this morning, but that I only have half an hour," I lied.

"I can't do that, Miss," he said. "Lieutenant Sabien, he said I was to give you five minutes to get dressed and if you wouldn't come, to drag you downtown as you are."

I closed the door quickly, unlatched the chain and opened the door, wider this time, giving him a good look at what he had only been guessing at.

"Do you have any idea how loud I would squawk if you dragged me anywhere like this?" I said. He swallowed hard and tried to look away. They really needed to start toughening these kids up. "By the time I was done crying to a review board, neither you nor Sabien would be cops anymore, that's for damn sure."

He was looking above my head, and doing it pretty resolutely. "I'll just have to take that chance, Miss," he said.

"All right, O'Doul," I said, "don't get rough. Come in."

"My name is Henderson, Miss," he said.

"I'll let you know if I start giving a damn," I said, closing the door behind him and picking up my piece from behind the door, which also seemed to startle him. Poor delicate flower of youth. "Have a seat in the front room, O'Doul. I'll be with you presently."

"Five minutes, Miss," he warned.

"In five minutes, O'Doul, I will be even less ready to go than I am now," I said, "and try to remember that I'm armed."

"Yes, Miss," he said, slumping ever so slightly.

I did not really require thirty-two minutes to get ready. If fact, I had to sit down and read a chapter of a paperback by my bedside in order to pass the time slowly enough to be a genuine pain in the backside, but not quite slowly enough for Officer Henderson to feel obligated to start rapping at my chamber door, which might give him the impression that he was in some way in control of the situation. At last I stepped out into the sitting room, where my erstwhile chaperone sat humbled with his hat in his hands and looking profoundly relived.

"Would you like some coffee?" I offered, mostly just to watch his face turn pale.

"No, Miss," he stammered. "We really don't have time to make any."

I made a small, pouty face. "Then we shall have to stop en route, O'Doul. We shall have to stop en route."

It is difficult to say exactly what displeased Lieutenant Sabien more, the timing of my arrival, the paper cup and danish in my hands or the lack of handcuffs on my wrists. Sabien was big on handcuffs. I suspected him of being a secret fetishist but had never kidded him on the point, mostly because I was certain that he would not blush like dear little Officer Henderson did.

Sabien eyed my danish with much the same unconcealed desire with which Henderson had been contemplating other delights back in my doorway. To each their own, though to be fair to Sabien, I was now wearing a much more conservative tweed suit.

"Is there anything else we can get for you, Princess?" he asked.

"No thanks," I smiled, nibbling a speck of icing off my thumb, "I'm just fine."

"These games are going to get you in trouble, Dixon," he said.

"You sound just like the Sisters," I smiled. "I know what I'm doing and you know that I do. That's what drives you crazy."

"What drives me crazy," he growled, "is that when you finally go too far and get yourself dead, it's me that's going to have to play whodunnit."

"Why Lieutenant Sabien," I purred, "I didn't know you cared."

"Shaddup," he said in a pretty decent simulation of disgust.

"You didn't send O'Doul in to drag me down here in my delicates to play guidance counselor, did you?" I asked.

"He didn't do much of a job of that, I see," Sabien said with a glare towards the wall of mirrors, suggesting my playmate was back there. I waggled my fingers hello and could almost feel him blush, though I couldn't see him.

"He talked rough," I said. "I had to teach him a lesson."

"One of these days somebody is going to teach you a lesson," Sabien said, "and it isn't gonna be us. God knows I've tried."

I looked at him and had a sudden revelation. "Sabien," I said, "you're way too young to have these kind of paternal feelings toward me."

Sabien's ears flushed ever so slightly and I knew that I had scored a hit for the very first time ever. "If you were my daughter, I'd turn you over my knee and give you a good spanking."

"Stop it," I said, "you're making me crazy."

Sabien slammed his hand down on the table in frustration. My paper cup jumped, but did not spill. I *picked it up and took a delicate sip as he thundered, "Damn it, Dixon, "can't you see when you're in over your head?"*

I played with my cup a little. "You don't scare me much, Sabien," I said.

"Believe it or not," he said, "I am the least of your problems. Though I am prepared to move up the list in a helluva hurry."

I officially lost my patience. "Just tell me what was so all-fired important that I had to scamper down here at six in the morning."

Sabien opened a file and threw a series of photographs down on the table in front of me. I did not look at them.

"If those are dirty pictures from Jimmy Lish's," I said, "I should warn you that I'm not in the mood anymore."

"Just look at them," Sabien said, in a voice that would bite me in half if it could.

I looked. It was Anne Mayfield. Dead. She was dressed more or less the way I was when Henderson had banged on my door. She was hanging from an exposed beam in a sitting room in the first couple of pictures. The rest had been taken after she had been cut down, and were mostly detail shots of the rope marks on her neck and some shots of what looked like bruising around her wrist. I put the pile down and looked back at Sabien.

"Yes?" I asked.

"Your client," Sabien said.

"Ex-client," I said.

"Whatever," he said with a shake of his head.

"Who did this?" I asked, trying to remain calm. If he saw that I was angry, he might get confused and think that I was scared.

"She did," he said, holding out a plastic bag with a piece of paper in it. "She left a note and everything."

I took the bag and read the note as best I could through the plastic, which I was clearly not invited to open. In it

she confessed to the murder of her husband's mistress
Janet Timms, and claimed to be unable to live with herself.
The note was typewritten, but signed, and it looked
genuine.

"This is bunk," I said, trying to sound certain.

"Typewriter was in the study," Sabien said. "The print
matches and the signature is right enough."

"A woman doesn't hang herself, Sabien," I said.

"Some do," he shrugged.

"Not this one. Some would do the head in the oven, but
that wouldn't be Anne Mayfield either," I said. "She
would be sleeping pills. A lot of them. And she would never
let you find her looking like that. She'd be horrified. She'd
have got dressed up in her finest and left a hand-written
note by her beautiful corpse."

Sabien snorted. "You know, the ones that take pills
usually vomit all over themselves at the end."

"Yeah," I said, "I know that. But they don't, and she
wouldn't."

"No, she wouldn't," he said.

"And if you thought she really killed herself," I said,
"or if you wanted me to think so, you wouldn't have left in
that picture of her wrist. Somebody grabbed her and held
her, hard, right?"

"Maybe," he said.

"So who did it?" I repeated.

"I have already been instructed," he said as quietly as
he ever said anything, "to use extreme discretion in tying
up loose ends in the matter of Anne Mayfield's tragic
suicide."

"You know it wasn't a suicide," I said.

"Nobody wants to hear it, Dixon," he said.

"You're not going to let that stop you," I said. It wasn't
really a question and he didn't take it as one.

"Nobody tells me to walk away," Sabien growled.
"Nobody. But it's gonna be quiet, so it's gonna take time."

"Why tell me?" I shrugged.

"Why do you think?" he asked. "This is a bad one. You're in trouble, Dixon."

"Trouble?" I asked. "This is stupid. Anne Mayfield hired me to get photographs of her husband and his mistress in action. She gives me the address and tells me they get down to business on Tuesdays. Then she heads over herself and kills Janet Timms in the one time and place when she can be absolutely certain that someone is watching. It's too stupid to live."

"Right," said Sabien. "Which means you weren't hired to take pictures at all, which is why there aren't any. You were hired to be a distraction. An alibi. Which makes you a co-conspirator."

"What?" I hollered. "That's idiotic!"

"It's enough to keep you in a cell for a while," Sabien said.

"Not if you want to keep this quiet," I said. "You think Molly Cameron won't sing to the press if I ask her to?"

"City Hall isn't the only thing keeping the papers quiet," Sabien said, "you think I don't know that? Right now you're the only person that can testify what Anne Mayfield did and said at your meeting. Which means you're the only one that can make the suicide sound like a fairy-tale. Which means the only place for you that's even remotely safe is a holding cell. Just until this blows over a little."

"Jesus Christ, Sabien," I said, "are you protecting me?"

"If you repeat it," he said, gathering up the photos, "I will deny it."

"I didn't ask for that and I don't want it," I said angrily. "You can't just barge into my life and throw me in a cell 'cause you reckon it's getting too dangerous."

"No," he said, "I can't. But we can play it that way for a couple of days and you can still be more or less alive at the end of this."

"I'm leaving now," I said.

"Think about what you're doing, Dixon," Sabien said without getting up. "Even if you make it out of this one, this little game doesn't have a happy ending. You keep this wise-guy routine up, you wind up a big zero, like your pal Black Jack. That guy has nothing, Dixon, and you could end up just like him."

"I am nothing like Jack Justice," I said, and opened the door leaving my danish to be scavenged by the wolves.

Chapter Twenty-Three

There was a knocking at my door. It would keep. The thing about knocking, or a ringing telephone, is that most people react to them like some sort of Pavlovian dog. They get exasperated when they are interrupted when it is they themselves that are doing the interrupting. I chose not to do so.

It was ten to eight. Many was the day when that time might find me sound asleep, or, in case that state should sound too healthful, at least powerfully unconscious. But not today. Sleep had been fitful and in the end, hunger had won out. I had neatly lifted the cap off my soft-boiled egg only four minutes ago, and I would not be rushed.

The knocking was persistent, I'd have to give it that. That alone was worthy of consideration. Most people would give up and go away, assuming that I was not home. Whomever was currently standing at my door seemed fairly certain that I was on the other side of it. They also seemed unprepared for the possibility that I would simply ignore them. I dipped another toast soldier in my egg. This was really the way to eat a soft-boiled egg, and usually I couldn't be bothered. Usually I boiled it a little too long and scooped the whole mess out onto a single piece of rye toast, buttered but uncut. Then I mashed it around with a fork and made a sort of open-faced sandwich. It was good. This was better. I dunked the toast in the egg again. I was getting down to the last of the yolk, which would mean it would be time to move on to stage two, scraping the inside of the shell out with a teaspoon to collect the egg white along the sides. This is how I ate them when I was a kid, and most of the time I was too grown-up to do it now even when no one was watching, which was almost all the time.

The knocking came again. It was heavier. Someone had either switched from using their knuckles to using the side of their fist, or been pushed aside by a companion who feared they might be doing it wrong. It seemed safest to assume the latter.

I looked at the coat pegs behind the door. My automatic was hanging there in its shoulder holster, precisely where I had taken it off last night. That seemed a little sloppy, though I had to admit it was the usual state of things. There was a loose floorboard in front of the door. It seemed unlikely that I could get to the gun without giving my proximity to the door away, which as of yet I did not wish to do.

I took the last bite of toast in egg, wiped my hands together to remove any offending crumbs and opened the breadbox. I did not keep bread in the breadbox. Not that it wasn't a good spot, but it tended to make a mess of the handgun I kept in there. It was a .38, with a nice balance and a good feeling in your hand. I didn't carry this one much anymore, I had become a fan of the big boom made by the .45, but this would do in a pinch.

The knock came again. I took another swallow of my coffee and considered digging the white out of the egg. I was uncertain of this, as it required two hands and some concentration, but I was standing in the kitchen with the counter between me and the open space of the front room, a nice clear sightline to the front door and a .38 special on the small ledge in front of me. I started digging out the egg. It was worth it.

The knock came again, louder this time. Trying hard to wake me up. It wouldn't be the landlord, he'd been paid. There were a few outstanding bills, but nothing worth sending some guys over for. Certainly not at eight in the morning. It could not be a friendly neighbour telling me to bring in my cat, as I had neither. Brush salesmen didn't work this early. Neither did door-to-door God salesmen. I put down the egg and the spoon. That was good.

This had been going on for five or six minutes now, which may not sound like a long time, but is, in fact, several minutes beyond much too persistent. Someone was quite sure that I was in here, and had been instructed to make some sort of contact with me. Cops would almost certainly have said something along the lines of *"Open Up! Police!"* by now. They couldn't be blamed, they had seen as many movies as I had, and couldn't help but fall into their roles as written. Besides, why would cops be at my door? I hadn't broken a single law since the last time I had seen them, which was actually pretty amazing by my standards.

The knocking had stopped. I waited. A moment later I heard the soft rattling of the doorknob. I smiled and went back to my coffee. I had a couple of minutes. One of the fringe benefits of knowing almost as much about lock-picking as the professionals is that you have a general idea of what you are looking for when shopping for a lock that will actually keep people out of your apartment. Nothing would keep out someone who was really good, but someone who was really good wouldn't have knocked for five minutes first. Neither would someone who wasn't an idiot, since everyone on my floor must now be awake and know that Jack Justice had visitors. I was briefly sorry for that, but it was about to get a whole lot louder.

Two minutes later there were three loud thumps at the door, different than the knocks had been. Someone had got frustrated and tried to kick the door in. This was fairly stupid, as the door actually opened out and there was a heavy frame that prevented exactly what they were trying. Was I going to have to actually let these boobs in? Another soft rattle told me that they had gone back to working the lock. Maybe I had time to get the automatic anyway. Maybe not. I finished my coffee and rinsed out the cup quietly.

There was a soft click from the doorway and I knew they were in at last. I picked up the .38. There was a light on in my bedroom and I knew that it would catch their eye first. Part of me wished that I had turned the shower on when the knocking started, but that would have precluded my enjoyment of the toast soldiers, and it didn't really matter. They were mine.

Two bulky shapes in overcoats crept in, their hats pulled low over their eyes. The first one would be cake. The second one might get a shot away and he might not. They certainly weren't expecting an armed response from the kitchenette. Trouble was, I didn't really have time for either of them to be dead right now. Or even crippled. Either option would turn my apartment into a crime scene, and that would tie me up for hours. If they were here, they were also elsewhere, and that meant that I had things to do.

The easiest shot in the world is a kill shot. Human beings keep almost all of their most precious organs in the same package, which is also the largest target on the human body. Center mass. The problem became once you had decided not to actually kill somebody, but not get killed yourself in the process. There were places you could hit a man and probably not kill him. Even places that made it fairly likely that he could retreat under his own power. But they were smaller targets. A handgun is not, whatever you might think, the world's most accurate weapon. It is very good for killing. Not killing is someone else's job. But today the .38 would have to do.

I pumped the first shot into the lead man's left shoulder. It came in a little high, and looked like it shattered the bone at the socket. This was good and bad. He went down like a sack of oatmeal, but I didn't really want him going into shock. His partner wheeled around and squeezed off two fast shots from a big automatic, but he had no idea what he was aiming at. Just an instant filled with something less than panic would have served him well, but it was not a lesson he would learn today. He had turned to face me, presenting me with the biggest target he possibly could. He was so clumsy he was practically moving in slow motion, like in the pictures. It was almost a shame not to kill him.

I put one into his right thigh and he wailed like a baby. I put a second one into his gun arm and he dropped his rod. He staggered toward the door shouting oaths as he did so, which would help to clear the hallway of eavesdropping neighbors if the gunplay hadn't already.

The first one was up again, or at least on his knees, twisting across his body to get a decent look at the kitchen counter where I had stood. I was not there any more, of course. I had stepped out of what the landlord had described when I saw the place as the "breakfast nook", and into the front room. In the process, I was almost behind the wounded thug, and the hole in his shoulder was presented to me as a gory mess. I brought my foot up and planted it solid into the wound. He howled and I used my gun to sledge him across the side of the head. Not too hard, Jack, don't want to put him out.

The blow staggered him, and I switched my pistol into my left hand and leaned over to take his. When the fog cleared from his eyes a second later, I had the .38 levelled in his face.

"Run," I said.

He ran.

There would be sirens soon. I had no time for this. I put on my shoulder holster and pulled my jacket over top. I put the .38 in one pocket and the gunsel's automatic in the other. I was now excessively well-armed. I grabbed my hat, thrust it on and pushed the door shut as I walked out. I heard the latch click and knew they had not broken my lock, which meant the cops probably would when they arrived. I took the service stairs down the back. Rossetti had soldiers watching my apartment long enough to be sure that I was there and then given the order. He was clearing up loose ends. That was fine. I had been a loose end before, and it looked like I would be again.

The street was dicey. If there had been more waiting down there, they might have given me trouble. I didn't know who and I didn't know where. But there was nothing. I had a moment's hesitation before starting my car, but if they were going to blow me up, why would they have tried to shoot me first? Mind you, after this it looked like it was taxis for a while. And me without an expense account.

The traffic was bad. I raced down side streets and alleys as best I could, but there was no way for me to get anywhere without hitting the morning rush from time to time. If they had gone to Trixie's apartment first, there wasn't much I could do about it. But she struck me as an "open-up-at-nine-on-the-dot" kind of girl, and I was hoping that Rossetti thought so too. So I headed for the office of the girl detective at the best speed I could make.

I pulled the car in sideways and sprinted for the door. If they were waiting for her outside I was completely exposed, and there wasn't much that I could do about that but get unexposed as quick as I could. I raced through the lobby and pounded up the stairs two at a time. When I hit her floor I opened the door and moved down the hallway quickly and silently, the way you only can when your life has depended upon both often enough not to think about it. Her door was closed, but it was pretty clear it had been forced, probably with a prybar. Not exactly a finesse job. The splinters had been hastily cleared away by whoever had done the job, but the frame was cracked. The latch probably wouldn't even catch. I wished I knew the layout of the room inside. I could expect two of them, that much seemed certain. One would be sitting at her desk chair, and that would almost certainly be right across from the door so she could greet potential clients the moment they came in. The other one could be anywhere, but the number of doors on this floor suggested that the offices themselves couldn't be big. One room. Take your shot, and make it your best. No more fancy shooting, Tex.

I kicked the door in and put the first shot into the brain of the one at the desk. He was a big one, and all set to smile when he got it. The second one was to the left, in the corner and with no cover. A swell spot if you plan to surprise a girl with her overcoat buttoned-up and no way to reach her hidden piece. A lousy spot for a gunfight. He got one away before I could turn to him, but he was in too much of a hurry and the round buried itself in the doorframe. He didn't get a second shot. I put two in his chest and he was gone before he hit the floor.

No sign of Trixie. Something must have held her up. I looked around the room. It had been trashed from top to bottom. What the hell could they have been searching for? Or was this all just calculated for effect? Put the scare into her, was that the point? I looked at the two gorillas and found it hard to believe that they would have put the point too delicately if that was indeed their plan. Besides, they were gangsters, they were armed, they were dead. I was in the clear, beyond the fact that this last point would drive Lieutenant Sabien into apoplexy.

Chapter Twenty-Four

I was reading the important safety notice pinned to the wall for the tenth time when Jack stepped out into the hall, and I still wasn't sure what it said. I had been on a slow burn for the last two hours and was still so mad that I was shaking.

"Hey," Jack said, surprised to see me.

"Hey yourself," I said, standing and seeing red as I did so. "Listen, Hotshot, I don't know what it is you're accustomed to, but I am not a fairy princess and I do not require rescuing, you follow that?" I was almost as surprised by this outburst as Jack. Until it happened, I didn't even know that I had intended to rip his head off. But there it was.

He didn't miss a beat though. "Who says I was riding to your rescue?" he snapped. "Maybe I went over to finally put you out of my misery, and shot two innocent hired killers by accident. Imagine my disappointment."

"Oh, yeah?" I hollered. Brilliant, Dixon. Nice retort.

"Yeah!" Jack said twice as loud as me.

"Pipe down!" a random voice from down the hall called out.

"Go to hell!" Jack and I replied, almost in unison and at top volume.

There was a moment of silence. I tried not to laugh, but it must have been obvious, because Jack rolled his eyes and pushed back a half-grin himself.

"Know what I think?" he asked. "I think the only people we hate more than each other right now is everybody else."

I nodded. "That sounds about right, actually," I said.

We didn't say anything for a minute.

"I'm sorry I took your head off," I said. "I don't know why I did that."

Jack shrugged. "Somebody just tried to kill us," he said, "and you didn't get to blow off any steam by shooting them like I did."

I nodded. "Two down, about a hundred and fifty to go," I said.

Jack nodded. "There are two others that'll be out of commission for a while, but otherwise that's probably about right. Mind you, that's the whole organization. Some of those wouldn't actually be muscle."

"Any chance of us living long enough to get to the accountants?" I asked.

Jack shrugged again. "I wouldn't think so," he said. "You been to your office?"

I shook my head. "The scene has been described to me in detail by your friend Sergeant Holm," I said.

"Ah, Ted," Jack smiled.

"Yeah," I said. "He tried pretty hard to be impressive, but he was also helpful. This way."

I started to walk through the corridors of Robbery-Homicide. To my surprise, Jack followed without protest.

"It isn't Ted's fault," Jack said, "he just has a weakness for a particular type."

"Jack," I said, "just about every man I meet has a weakness for my particular type."

"Nice to see it hasn't gone to your head," Jack snorted.

"No," I said, "but it does make it tough to take any of you seriously." I opened a door at the far end of the hall and headed down a set of stairs, as Sgt. Holm had showed me earlier.

Jack followed. "What about Big Al Rossetti?" Jack said, his voice echoing down the staircase. "Are we taking him seriously yet?"

"Oh, we are indeed," I said. "He started to clean house earlier than we thought."

"I noticed that," Jack replied. "Where in the hell are we going?"

"Motorpool," I replied.

"Why are we going to the motorpool?" Jack asked.

"Trying not to pick up a tail the second we leave the station," I replied. "On account of I would like to live a little longer and am unwilling to hide in police headquarters for the next month or so."

"Nice," he said. "Your office was pretty trashed."

"So I hear," I replied.

"They were looking for something," Jack said.

"Yes," I said.

"What were they looking for?" Jack asked.

I opened the door into the underground car bay. The loading dock was quiet, and there weren't more than a half a dozen officers all milling about on what appeared to be legitimate business. I could see my car down at the end near the ramp to the street. I reached into my handbag and gripped the Beretta. "My best guess is they were looking for my camera," I said.

"Your camera?" Jack asked.

"Yes," I said. "'Cause your office wasn't touched."

"I see two problems with that," Jack replied.

"Only two?" I asked.

"There isn't anything on your camera," he said, ignoring me. "Nothing of Mayfield or Timms, anyway."

"I know that," I said. "But they couldn't be sure."

"Also your camera is at my office," he said.

I nodded. "Yeah, remind me to kill you for that later," I said. "I guess that means whoever their source is isn't that close to the case."

"A dirty cop?" Jack said. "You astonish me."

"Yeah, well, keep your eyes peeled, Geronimo," I said, still eying the officers who shared the underground with us. "This would be a pretty stupid place to die."

"It's an interesting point," he said. "If you're right, this is the first thing that ties Rossetti to Jimmy Lish's murder."

"Beyond our cunning brand of guesswork?" I offered.

"Yeah," he said, "besides that. If Rossetti is on the hunt for photos, it means that Lish had something Rossetti thought was worth killing for. Or at least Rossetti thought he did."

"Doesn't do us much good," I said. "He's got it now."

"Does he?" Jack asked. "If Lish had pictures of Mayfield's extracurricular activities, would he have been stupid enough to keep them in his office? All of them?"

I stopped beside my car. "Would Jimmy Lish really have been worried about reprisals from Roger Mayfield?" I asked.

"What if Mayfield wasn't the target?" Jack asked, with a tone of sudden revelation.

"What?" I spat.

"Rossetti asks Janet Timms to make Mayfield happy and keep him that way. She doesn't know why, but she figures he rates. Maybe she contacts Lish, maybe it was Lish's idea, who knows, but they decide Rossetti owes Janet a little more for her years of service."

"Oh my God, they're idiots," I said.

"They are also dead," Jack agreed.

"They set up the photo shoot and went to Big Al looking for a payout?" I asked.

Jack shrugged. "Could be," he said.

"So how did Mayfield get the photo?" I asked.

"Maybe they sent it to him to shake him up," Jack said. "Let him deliver the news to Rossetti. Or maybe Janet Timms had a stack of prints made up to present to Big Al and Mayfield discovered them. Took the one that showed the least of his skin and brought it to me."

"Which would explain the 'no demands'," I said. "He didn't know for sure what was going on, but he knew how dead he was if he became a liability to Rossetti."

Jack thought about it. "Seems a little too cunning for Roger Mayfield," he said, "but it could be. Anyway, the precise chronology isn't that important."

"Except in court," I said, "which looks to be the only way we live through this."

"Okay, point," Jack said. "But it means that Jimmy Lish's prize petunias might still be out there somewhere and if we had them, we might have something to bargain with."

"Yeah," I said. "That worked out well for Janet Timms."

Jack nodded and looked around. "Were we going somewhere?" he asked.

"We were," I said, "but we're here now."

"Where?" he asked.

"Here," I said, pointing to my car.

"Whose car is this?" he asked.

"You're a real dim bulb, you know that, Justice?" I said.

"Explain," he said.

"It's my car, dingus," I said, "we've been using yours and it isn't safe."

"How did it get here?" Jack frowned.

"Your friend Ted went and got it," I said, "while you were having tea and cookies with Sabien."

"Ted went above and beyond," Jack said with a smirk.

"Stop smiling, idiot," I said. "I saw the wedding band. Miss Dixon does not cross that particular line."

"He'll be crushed," Jack said.

"Only if you tell him," I said. "Cops who get your car for you are much too useful to let off the hook that easily."

"I'll bet," Jack said. "It beats walking home."

"Especially when there's probably a car full of shooters waiting out front," I agreed. "Get in."

"You're driving?" he asked.

I looked at him across the hood of my car. "You have exactly six seconds to retract that question entirely," I said, "or I will shoot you in the knee and leave you here for Sabien or Rossetti."

Jack thought about it for five seconds. "That's tough, but fair," he said.

Chapter Twenty-Five

The door to the back room opened and Mickey Fetz walked in. At least, I assumed it was Fetz. He was just as I had pictured him after we spoke on the phone. He was thin to the point of being wiry and he fidgeted constantly, as if he didn't sit right in his own skin. The skin itself had that grey pallor that it often took on after a long stretch inside, but Freddie hadn't mentioned anything about Fetz being a jailbird, and Freddie usually would. To most of the criminal underclass, an occasional stretch of hospitality of the state was just an occupational hazard. My old pal Freddie the Finger, on the other hand, regarded such a thing as pure voodoo. Bad luck which tended to be contagious when you had an ex-con around. He worked with them, of course. Swimmers in the shallow end of the talent pool don't always get to pick and choose their playmates. But he always knew which ones they were, and made sure not to get too close to them. If a man got caught once, Freddie reasoned, he's a bad risk to repeat.

But Freddie hadn't pegged Mickey Fetz as a con, which meant either Freddie didn't know or Fetz picked up his clammy, corpse-like appearance by other means. I watched him fidget as he made his way over to Trixie and I. Maybe a hop-head. I trust those less than cons.

Freddie had got the word out for us that we were looking for whoever might have taken over Jimmy Lish's casebook. He had done it fast and on the sly, and taken a certain amount of risk doing so. All the same, after setting up the meeting with Fetz, Freddie advised me that he'd be out of town for a couple of weeks, just in case word should get to Mr. Rossetti who in some way might misinterpret the request. Freddie was not particularly valiant, and with guys like Al Rossetti, that was a pretty healthy approach.

The back room at the Green Stripe had been Fetz's call. It was surprisingly large for the management to allow it to be used for a small private party like this, but it was still early in the day and my guess was they knew Fetz here.

About ten feet away from the table where the girl detective and I sat, Mickey Fetz took on a different manner. He smiled and it seemed to spread throughout his whole person, like an oil slick on top of water. His hesitant, squirrel-like manner softened into a smooth approach, full of self-confidence. It was a hell of an act, and I might have bought it if he had turned it on before he walked in the room. We didn't stand as he approached.

He licked his lips before he spoke, like a lizard. "Mister Dutton?" he asked.

I nodded. He sat.

"It's interesting," he said, "there is no Harold Dutton in the city directory."

"Who says I'm from the city?" I said.

Fetz shrugged and smiled. He made an extravagant little gesture with his left hand, as if sweeping the matter of my mysterious identity away.

"If you knew something was fishy," Trixie said, "why did you come?"

Fetz leaned back in his chair and considered Trixie as though he was having trouble focusing on her. "Sweetie, in my business, everyone and everything is fishy. I still have got to eat." He lit a cigarette delicately and smiled. He looked from Trixie to me and back again.

"So," he said, a smile quivering about his lips, which he licked again, "you two had business with Jimmy?"

I nodded.

"He didn't have pictures of either of you," Fetz said. "I've been through his stock very carefully, and I think I would remember."

It could have been my imagination, but that seemed to be a little more directed toward me than it was Trixie.

"How well did you know Jimmy Lish?" I asked.

Fetz shrugged. "Well enough," he smiled. "Guys in my line of work don't make a lot of friends, but Jimmy was a solid guy. It's a damn shame, what happened to him."

"What did happen to him?" asked Trixie, as if she didn't know.

Fetz licked his lips again and twisted his neck, as if stretching it, never taking his eyes off us as he did so. "What can I say?" he asked. "It seems that Jimmy had a dissatisfied customer. One that wasn't bright enough to realize there wasn't anything important in his shop."

"I hear some stuff was stolen," I said plainly.

Fetz snorted. "Sure," he said, "I hear that too. But there wasn't anything in the files that could have been important to you. Unless you'd done some work with Jimmy for the skin mags, but you don't strike me as the type." Fetz grinned. That one was definitely to me. "That's how we met, Jimmy and me. He was just getting started then, and I showed him the ropes. Showed him how he could use that camera of his to make some real money. But Jimmy loved the dance. He loved girls, loved luring them in under the pretence of art shots, loved convincing them to do a little more, and then a little more, until he had seen it all. But it's a labor-intensive process. If you figure it out, the hourly rate is pathetic."

"Gosh," Trixie said, "that's a shame."

"Don't be like that," Fetz scolded. "They have their fun too. Besides, I'd bet my last dollar you weren't one of them."

"Why is that?" Trixie asked.

Fetz beamed a wise and beneficent smile at Trixie. "Ah," he said, licking his lips again, "that would be telling." My guess was that Lish liked his girls young and farm fresh, and then he broke them. Trixie was neither farm fresh nor broken. I didn't feel like saying so any more than Mickey Fetz did.

"Did you know Janet Timms?" I asked, returning the conversation to something I cared about.

"Janet?" Fetz was contemptuous. "Sure. Jimmy did some work with her. A little photography, but then he brought her in to the real work. She was swell bait. He made some real good money, then he made the mistake of falling for her. What a maroon."

There was real mockery in Fetz's voice, as if falling for Janet Timms was the most absurd thing he could imagine. "You don't think she was worth it?" I asked.

"You don't take your own bait," Fetz hissed. "It isn't done. That one cost Jimmy a lot of grief, but in the end he couldn't betray his nature. He kept all of his hobbies, and Janet didn't like him playing with others, so it ended. They're still friendly, I guess." A thought occurred to him. "You two aren't from Janet, are you?"

"What if we are?" I said.

"Forget it," Fetz said, with a smile and a shake of his head. "Stupid question. Janet knew that Jimmy and I had an understanding about our caseloads. If she had any expectations about their last job, she'd have come right to me."

"What would you have told her?" Trixie asked.

"I'd have told her that any deal she had with Jimmy died with him," Fetz said, the smile fading and the twitches starting to return. He stroked his left eyebrow delicately, as if calming himself. "I'd have given her the same rate I pay to any bait I use, and if she didn't like it she could go to hell. And if you are from her, you can tell her that yourselves."

"Janet Timms is dead," I said, breaking up his rhythm.

"Dead?" Fetz was quiet. "When?"

"Couple of days," I said.

"I didn't hear anything," Fetz protested.

"It's being kept quiet," Trixie said.

"By who?" Fetz was getting angry, like we were pulling his leg.

"By the same people who did the killing," I said. "The same people that killed Jimmy Lish."

I wouldn't have thought that Fetz could turn more grey, but he did.

"Who?" he said at last.

"Rossetti," I said.

Fetz looked from me to Trixie to me again. He looked like he was going to have an accident.

"We aren't from Rossetti either," Trixie said, sensing the same thing.

"No," I said. "But it's just a matter of time."

"That stupid little tramp," Fetz cursed, almost at a whisper. There were tears in his eyes and he looked like he might break down entirely. "That stupid, stupid little tramp."

"Timms?" I asked.

Fetz nodded. "I've been trying to figure what it was that made this Mayfield guy such a big deal. Jimmy was sure it was a big one. The score to end them all."

"Jimmy was getting too big for his britches," Trixie said.

"No," Fetz protested. "No, Jimmy would never have done something stupid like try and hit up Big Al. As far as he was concerned Mayfield was the mark."

"And where did he figure the money was coming from?" I asked.

"He didn't ask," Fetz spat. "Janet brought the job to him, cut him in. She'd done all the setup already. Jimmy was excited, he was happy to be working with her again. He was proud that she showed the initiative. All that crap."

"Why would he get into something like this without knowing the whole shot?" Trixie asked.

"What was to know?" Fetz practically shrieked. "'Hey pal, pay up or Mrs. Mayfield gets the whole photographic essay.' That's the job. But he was so soft on that broad. Still, after everything, soft on her. Said she was like candy, once you'd had a taste, you'd always want it again. And besides, they made big money together."

"Not big enough, I guess," Trixie said.

"That stupid little tramp," Fetz cursed again.

"And who else is stupid, Fetz?" I asked. "You get word through the grapevine that somebody wants a meet with whoever owns Jimmy Lish's back catalogue, and you set this up in an hour. You walk in here, knowing damn well that you've got a phony name and not much else. How many other people know about you and Jimmy, Fetz?"

"Oh Jesus Christ," he wailed softly, the tears starting to flow.

"None of that," I snapped. "There isn't time."

"That stupid little tramp," he practically whispered.

"The way I figure it is this," I said. "Whoever killed Lish took everything they could find in his files on Janet Timms. Walked out with a box full of prints. Sooner or later, Rossetti goes through it to make sure that his boys got the Mayfield pictures, and when he finds that they didn't, he does just exactly what we did. He puts out the word, and it leads him to you."

"We want everything on the Mayfield job," Trixie said. "All of it."

"Why should I?" Fetz whimpered.

"'Cause if you don't give it to me," I said, "I'll make nice with Big Al by calling him and telling him that you've got it."

Fetz stared at me wildly, with empty, panicked eyes.

"What if I do the same to you," Fetz said, "after I give you the pictures?"

I shrugged. "Good luck with that, Mickey," I said. "Now get on your feet."

Chapter Twenty-Six

I don't know why it should surprise me that there are now high-rise buildings made for nothing but parking cars in, but it still does. I know of three of them, in fact, the one out behind the City Hall administration offices being the tallest of them. Seven stories of artificial road inside the building, with row after row of nearly identical cars parked by equally identical civil servants. The wave of the future.

This kind of place is tough to get into if you aren't in the right car with the right pass to display to the little man in the peaked cap who sits at the entrance and works the barrier. Show him the correct piece of paper from your driver's-side window and he will smile and admit you into the paradise of multi-level parking. Fail to do so and he will scowl and point you away as if you were an insect. Oddly enough, if you aren't in a car at all, you can just walk past him as if he wasn't there. No one else seemed to be doing it, but if you didn't come to park, you didn't compute to the little man. Black Jack and I strode past him and walked around the faceless grey mass of concrete until we found the plates that we were looking for.

It was half past four. Hopefully Roger Mayfield would not decide to work late, but even if he did, ol' Square Jaw and I seemed almost invisible to the pedestrians who entered from the covered walkway on the level above and searched for their own cars with the same bleary-eyed determination with which we had found Mayfield's.

Between ten to five and quarter past, the floodgates opened and the parked cars up and down the seven levels sprang to life almost as one and settled into a nice, slow piece of gridlock just like the one that waited for the drivers when they hit the city streets. And through it all, in the ever-building haze of exhaust fumes, Jack and I stood and waited, leaning against a pillar conspicuously.

At least I felt conspicuous. Indeed, I felt ridiculous, the only humans in a sea of man/car hybrids, trying to look like a pair of sightseers. I half expected to see a prowl car pull up for us at any moment, but none ever arrived. Perhaps we were less interesting than I believed. Or perhaps the commuters could not be bothered to stop and raise an alarm about a pair of his and hers malingerers.

In any event, by five thirty-three, the improbable building was quiet again, Jack and I were undisturbed and Roger Mayfield was on his way down the ramp toward his car at last. It occurred to me in that moment that he had come to work on the day that his wife was found to have committed suicide. What a trouper.

He walked quickly, but without fear. We would have to fix that.

"Mister Mayfield," Jack called as he approached, and the 'mister' notwithstanding, Mayfield's jump made it clear that he was not as unconscious of his plight as he seemed. When he realized who it was, he didn't seem to know if he ought to be relieved or annoyed.

"You again," he snapped. "I thought I told you to stay away."

"Yes, sir," Jack said. "You did say that. But it seemed impractical."

"I could have you arrested," Mayfield said. "I could have you charged with harassment."

"You could," Jack said. "But you would have to explain to the police and probably a judge why talking to you in a parking lot qualifies as harassment. I think they'd be very interested in that argument, don't you, Trixie?"

"Very," I said. "Even more interested in the visual aids we could bring to the party."

Mayfield seemed alarmed by this, but said nothing. He looked from me to Jack.

"That's right, Mayfield," Jack said. "Jimmy Lish's final job. We could take it over if we wanted."

"I don't know what you're talking about," he said.

"Nobody has to see them, Mayfield," Jack said. "Nobody knows we've got them. But it's time for you to come clean about Big Al Rossetti."

Mayfield looked like he had been struck. "I don't know anyone by that name," he said.

"He doesn't know anyone by that name, Trixie," Jack said without looking at me.

"Isn't that adorable?" I asked. "He's playing tough."

"You two don't scare me," Mayfield said. "You don't know a thing."

"We know a thing or two, Mayfield," I said. "And what we don't know doesn't matter all that much. We don't know if Rossetti used Janet Timms to get close to you, or if she was your down payment, or if she was just supposed to keep you happy for a while. We don't know that. But we do know that you were doing the mattress dance with the retired property of one of the city's most notorious gang leaders. We also know that he is the man who stands to profit the most from re-routing the Long Branch Expressway through Riverton. Millions of dollars in government money, Mister Mayfield, and you were the key to it all. You can make him legitimate at a stroke of a pen. We know that much."

"You don't know anything," Mayfield spat. "This is innuendo. Slander. I'll sue the both of you."

"Oh dear," I said. "He'll sue us, Jack."

"He'll have to dig up our corpses first," Jack said grimly. "We're in the middle of this, Mayfield, and you put us here. You came to me when you found out about the pictures. You didn't go to your new best friend Rossetti. You tried to clean it up on the quiet, like a smart guy. You bought my life for thirty dollars a day, and if you didn't know that you were killing me in the process than you're a bigger idiot than you'd have to be to think that a girl like

Janet Timms could ever get hot for you if she weren't
ordered to."

"That's a lie!" Mayfield howled like wounded animal.
"Janet loved me! It wasn't her fault. You have no idea
what she'd been through. Trapped between men like
Rossetti and Lish. She did what she did, but she did it for
us!"

Jack and I looked at each other. "And how is that
working out for you so far, Mister Mayfield?" I asked.

"You two have no idea," he said, "no idea what these
people are capable of."

"We have a pretty good idea," Jack said. "This woman
that you loved, that you still love. Doesn't matter if she
was selling you out, bleeding you white or as innocent as
the new-driven snow. Doesn't matter who's right,
Mayfield. She's dead."

Mayfield held a long-supressed sob from somewhere
deep within. He held it in, but only just. Jack didn't stop.

"They put a bullet in her head, Mayfield," he said,
"and at this point it doesn't matter if they did it because
she tried to blackmail Big Al Rossetti, or if they just
thought that she might. It doesn't matter at all."

"It matters to me!" Mayfield cried.

"It won't make her less dead," Jack said. Mayfield lost
his battle with the sob, which burst forth in a sudden gasp
and threatened to bring its brothers along. Jack kept right
on pushing. "She's dead because your new friends killed
her. Do they deserve your loyalty?"

Mayfield's eyes were full of tears. He was on the ropes.

"They killed Jimmy Lish," I said, "and his job was
keeping quiet after he'd been paid. They killed him
because he was a loose end, and they can't have any more
loose ends. If you attract too much attention to yourself
and blow the Riverton deal, the entire Rossetti family
fortune is tied up in worthless real estate. They killed your
wife, for Christ's sake. Your wife, who trusted you.

Whatever problems you had before Janet Timms made her entrance, you loved her once. They framed her and murdered her. Does that mean nothing to you?"

"You don't understand," Mayfield was weeping now. "Anne was furious. She said she'd go to the papers, go to the police, she just wanted to hurt me."

"And they protected you by hanging her," I said. Mayfield was trembling now, and he looked like he might vomit.

"What am I supposed to do?" Mayfield said. "I'm in too deep already."

"Not yet," Jack said. "You're not in too deep as long as you're alive. They've gone a long way to try and shield you in this, Mayfield. But once the final vote is taken and the Expressway is headed up Magee and Jefferson, who's left that can hurt them? Do you really think they'll give you a chance?"

"You're just trying to scare me," Mayfield said, pulling himself together.

"If you're not scared yet, Mayfield, you're too stupid to still be alive," Jack growled. "There's only one way out of this that involves you still walking on this Earth in a month. Come downtown with us and tell the police what you know."

"Why do you care?" Mayfield whimpered.

"Because we're in this up to our necks, Mayfield," Jack said, "and you're the one that put us there."

"So?" Mayfield said. "Why not just take the pictures to the police yourself? Why do you need me?"

"Because that's what we do, Mister Mayfield," I said. "You'll never understand this, so I'll try it once and then forget it. We're private detectives. We act on someone's behalf. It isn't enough to save our own skins. We'll do it that way if we have to, but it isn't what we do. This is how we enter the story, this is how we see it through."

Mayfield stared at me dumbly and looked to Jack.

"Don't look at me," Jack said. "I never argue with her when she's right."

"Mister Rossetti will protect me," Mayfield said with a shake of his head, backing away toward his car. "He'll protect me and he will reward me for my loyalty."

Mayfield opened his door and jumped into the car, firing the starter as he did so. "You'll see," he called as he pulled out quickly. "It isn't me who's dead. It's the two of you!"

He stepped on the gas and peeled away, down the endless turn that took him back to the street.

"What do we do?" I asked. "Go after him?"

Jack said nothing, but just stood and listened to Mayfield's engine racing down the levels.

"He's going too fast," Jack said quietly.

An instant later there was a loud crash and Jack and I sped down the exit ramps on foot as quickly as we could. Mayfield's car had slammed into the wall between the second and ground floors. The frame was crumpled and the windshield was smashed from the inside out. By the time we rounded the corner, black smoke was already pouring out, and the interior of the car was licked with bright red tongues of flame. A small crowd of six or seven passers-by, including the guard with the peaked cap, were all clustered around desperately searching for any sign of life and seeing none. We stood at the top of the ramp and got no closer.

"They cut his brakes," I offered.

"Yes they did," Jack agreed. "He probably panicked and stomped on the gas when they didn't work. Sounds crazy, but that's how it happens sometimes."

"Maybe," I shrugged. "But they also rigged the car to burn. Look at that. There's no reason for the interior to burn first unless someone meant for it to."

"Yeah," Jack agreed. "Dammit."

"Think any of that will show up in the accident report?" I asked.

Jack shook his head. "Despondent after the tragic suicide of his beloved wife," he said. "Rossetti must figure it's a bigger risk leaving him breathing than to wait for the final vote."

"Think we can stop the vote?" I asked.

Jack shrugged. "No," he said. "Not without Mayfield. Rossetti probably owns enough votes on the city council to get it through as it is."

"You realize there are only two loose ends left," I said.

"Yeah," said Jack. "Come on."

We walked away as unobtrusively as we could, before the law arrived.

"We need a client," Jack said.

"What for?" I asked.

"For what you said," Jack replied simply. "That was the most sense you've ever made in my presence, don't louse it up now."

"For Pete's Sake, Jack," I said, "couldn't we just focus on staying alive?"

Jack shook his head as we walked back toward my car. "If the only thing I'm working for is to save my own neck," he said, "I'm not at all sure that it's worth it."

I thought about this, and decided not to argue.

Chapter Twenty-Seven

Trixie pushed the door of Spenser's Place open and breezed in like she owned the joint. I followed behind, bouncing the door off my shoulder as my hands were full. In the right I held the .45, always reliable. In the left, I gripped the .38 I had taken from the breadbox this morning. It had spent the interval in my pocket and I thought it might as well get in on the fun. I couldn't actually fire both at the same time with any degree of accuracy, but I looked damn good holding them both, and since it was profoundly not my intent to shoot anyone just now, looks were what mattered. Anyone who had ever seen a western or read an adventure book would know I was no one they wanted to play with.

Hap Spenser jumped when he saw us, but I thrust the .38 toward him and he froze right enough. The rest of the barflies were all to my right, and they seemed plenty impressed with the .45.

"Hands on the bar," I said. "Do it."

They did it. They didn't like it or understand it, but they did it.

"Where I can see them, Mister Spenser," I said. "Please."

"Please and everything," Hap Spenser snorted. I really hoped he didn't go for his gun. I'd feel like an idiot shooting this guy. He kept his hands above the bar. I lowered my gun arm.

"Mister Spenser," Trixie said, all business, "you almost certainly do not realize this, but my associate Mister Justice and myself are in the middle of an uncomfortable situation just now."

"Is that a fact?" Hap Spenser said, quite lost.

"We are, as you may have gathered, private detectives," Trixie said.

Hap nodded slowly, as if reluctant to agree to anything.

"Without belaboring the events of the last seventy-two hours too much," Trixie said with something like a sigh, "it is fair to say that we have been put into a situation by a pair of clients, one of whom was certainly more aware of the full implications than the other. I digress. What was supposed to have been variations on a simple divorce job now has us thrust right into the middle of the Riverton expressway, with a strong probability of being run over by the Rossetti crime family."

This got Hap's attention at least.

"Rossetti's tried to buy you out?" Trixie asked.

"He tried to burn me out last night," Hap said. "I got a piece of one of them."

Trixie nodded. "He's running out of time," she said. "You were right, Rossetti is the one that bought up Riverton and let it rot. He did it because he knew there was a chance the Long Branch would run though here and knew that he could manipulate events to ensure that it did. Every cent his holding companies get from the Government for these buildings will be as thoroughly laundered as it could be."

. Hap Spenser sighed, like a balloon deflating a little. Hearing someone else say it like it was a fact seemed to be a relief to him. "So why does he need my place so bad?"

"He doesn't," Trixie said. "Aside from the fact that he's a stubborn man, with a tendency to take whatever he wants."

"He offered me peanuts," Spenser said in a low voice. "If he had offered me even a half-fair price for a run-down place in a half-deserted neighborhood, I might have taken it. But he would rather insult me. And when I found out who was in the back of it I swore he'd never get my place. He poisoned Riverton. Killed it slow, and did it for nothing. But he doesn't get my place."

"That's fair," Trixie said. "We would like to represent your interests in this matter."

Now Hap Spenser really was confused. "You how much?" he said.

Trixie continued. "Neither Mister Justice nor myself are currently employed by the clients who brought us into this matter," she said, "and in all fairness that is at least partly because both of them are dead, though in our defense, that only happened after they had terminated our employment."

"Naturally," Hap said, his leathery face a mask of wonder.

"We have, through the pursuit of our previous clients' interests, unwittingly been brought into conflict with the Rossetti family," Trixie said. "A confrontation seems at this point to be inevitable, and we would like it to be in the name of something other than simple survival. Although we are not opposed to that either."

"Of course," Hap said.

"There are two common threads that link everyone whom we have met in the course of this investigation," Trixie said. "Number one, we despise almost all of them, present company excepted. We like you."

"I'm so glad," said Hap, still baffled by it all.

"And number two, most of them are dead, again present company excepted," Trixie smiled. "I should add that we have, thus far, killed very few of them, though I expect that will have to change, and soon. In any event, we find ourselves in need of a client. The need is more a moral one than a financial one, though naturally that does exist as well. For our combined services, we are prepared to offer you a rate of thirty-five dollars a day, and on this occasion we will forgo the expenses."

Hap looked from her to me and back again. "Do you two drum up a lot of business this way?"

"Steady stream," I said.

"I should be clear, Mister Spenser," she said, ignoring the levity. "Mister Justice and I do not feel it is very likely that anything we do will stop the final vote on running the expressway through Riverton. This is just too big, and too many people have a piece of it. But if we are able to do so, we will stop Rossetti's efforts to gain control of your place before the expropriations begin. You will get a fair price for your place, and maybe a little more."

Hap sighed, and a lot of him seemed to leave his body with it. He looked old for the first time. "They killed Riverton a long time ago," he said. "The place I knew is long gone, and all the people too. My pension is in this bar. I have to get something."

"Yes, sir," Trixie said.

"Thirty-five, you said?" Hap Spenser asked.

"Yes, sir," Trixie nodded, opening her handbag and producing an receipt book. "Normally we would ask you for three days in advance at the outset of a job, but as it seems fairly unlikely that we will live longer than twenty-four hours, we are prepared to leave it at thirty-five."

"You two have kind of a funny way about you, you know that?" he asked.

"Yes, sir," Trixie said, "we know. It's been working so far."

Spenser seemed intrigued. "How can you tell?" he asked.

Trixie smiled. "We're the only ones not dead," she said.

Hap Spenser opened the cash register and took out two tens and three fives, which he handed to the girl detective. She sat at the bar and wrote him out a receipt, nice and official. Then they shook hands. Hap looked at me and I nodded. I was still holding a lot of guns.

Thirty seconds later, we were back out in the chill of the night.

"Okay," she said, handing me a ten and a five, which did not escape notice, "now what?"

"Now we make a deal," I said grimly.

Chapter Twenty-Eight

Anthony Brazzi was a big man, at least six-foot four, though he looked still taller in the immaculately tailored grey suit that he wore. He was pulling the tie off when he entered the room and turned on the light, revealing Black Jack and I waiting for him in the darkness.

He looked at us for a moment, saying nothing. "What if my family had been home?" he asked.

"We'd have done this somewhere else," Jack said.

Brazzi nodded. "Well," he said, "do it and be on your way."

Jack and I exchanged a look.

"I don't think you quite understand what's going on here," Jack said.

Brazzi's brows knit. "You aren't from Chick Mason?"

"No, sir," I said, "but I can see how you might make that mistake."

"Chick Mason is the only gang leader in town crazy enough to use women as gunsels," Brazzi said, giving me the up and down with his eyes. Cheeky, even in the face of doom. I like that in a man.

"We aren't from Chick Mason," Jack repeated, "and we aren't here to do you any harm. We're independent operators and we're here to negotiate."

Brazzi instantly became the most important man in the room again, though he had never felt like he was far off.

"Well," he said, "you aren't off to the very best of starts, but I'll listen while you talk. Will you have a drink?"

"No, sir," Jack said. "Please feel free to make yourself one, but bear in mind that I would find it seriously inconvenient to have to shoot you. It is nowhere in my plans, and I would ask that you not put it on the table."

"That seems fair," Brazzi said.

"You're Anthony Brazzi," Jack said. "Number two man in the Rossetti organization."

"Is that a question?" Brazzi smiled as he made his way to the small but impressively stocked bar on the sideboard.

"It is not," Jack said. "Security is kind of light here, sir, if you don't mind my saying."

"I don't mind at all," Brazzi said. "And you're right. Mister Rossetti has been an advocate of letting reputation and fear be our protectors, rather than appear to live in an armed camp."

"Mister Rossetti has protection," Jack offered.

"Mister Rossetti is the boss," Brazzi said with a smile. "But your little stunt tonight will give me an excuse to increase security. I suppose I ought to thank you."

Jack nodded. "Yes, sir," he said.

Brazzi considered Jack a moment. He seemed to have forgotten about me, but part of me was sure that he hadn't, that he saw every move I made, like a rattler waiting to strike.

"You're very well mannered," Brazzi said. "Who are you?"

"Jack Justice," Jack said, rather pointedly not introducing me, which given how far out on a limb we were, was probably not the worst thing he ever did.

Brazzi repeated the name under his breath before finally finding it in his memory. "You're that Private Detective. From the Riverton thing." Brazzi said nothing to me, but looked over and took the length of me in again. He knew who I was, all right.

"Yes, sir," I said, "the Riverton thing. Or as some would call it, the murders of Janet Timms, Jimmy Lish and Anne and Roger Mayfield."

Brazzi smiled. "I wouldn't know anything about that."

"No, sir," I said. Brazzi looked back to Jack.

"If you're here to ask for your lives, you're asking the wrong man. This whole Riverton project is Big Al's baby. He's been at it for years, as long as I can remember." Brazzi twirled his cocktail in his hand. "The fact that Janet

is dead should tell you how seriously he takes this. He still loved her. After that... well, he got a little crazy. But it's the kind of crazy that got him where he is today."

"Yes, sir," Jack said. "And now he's ready to throw it all away."

Brazzi seemed startled, but said nothing.

"Lots of guys in Rossetti's line dream about going legit," Jack said, "but it never happens. Sometimes it's too complicated, sometimes there's too much money to hide, or too many old scores to settle. Sometimes they just never get the chance. But this Riverton deal, this could finally do it, couldn't it?"

Brazzi nodded coolly. "It could," *he said.*

"So where does that leave you?" Jack asked.

"I beg your pardon?" Brazzi said.

"Most of the muscle, the low-level operators, they'll catch on with another outfit somewhere," Jack said with a smile. "But guys like you? Guys who have spent a lifetime climbing the ladder in the organization, where do you go? Who else would trust you?"

Brazzi spoke calmly and without emotion. "Mister Rossetti has been very clear that we will be taken care of. He wants to bring us into his legitimate organization."

Jack snorted. "As what?" *he asked.* "Are you going to have an office, Mister Brazzi? And a secretary?"

"Doesn't sound that bad, does it?" Brazzi smiled.

"Maybe not at first," Jack said. "But the real work will be done by Mister Rossetti and a bunch of investment bankers. Are you actually going to have a job to do, or is he supposed to support all of you indefinitely? And the more legit he gets, the less he's going to trust the den of career criminals he's keeping as pets."

Brazzi said nothing.

"And the longer this goes on, the more the Rossetti territory gets carved up by the city's other gangs," Jack said. "They won't sit around and wait for Rossetti to finish *playing businessman. At the first sign of weakness they'll be in like jackals. It's already beginning, isn't it? You thought the Mason gang was stepping in and taking you out."*

"None of this matters, Justice," Brazzi snapped. "It isn't my decision."

"Yeah," said Jack, "but what if it was?"

There was a long pause. Brazzi took a drink.

"What are you suggesting, Mister Justice?" he asked.

"I am suggesting that this whole business with the expressway was bad news from the start," Jack said. "I am suggesting that Mister Rossetti has been only thinking of himself, and that means he doesn't deserve the loyalty of his organization. I am further suggesting that it is only a matter of time before someone else comes to this same conclusion and feels like they have to deal with you as well to clear the path to the throne."

Brazzi shook his head and smiled.

"Miss Dixon and myself are the last two pieces of unscortched Earth between Rossetti and his dream," Jack said. "We didn't declare war on Al Rossetti, he declared it on us."

Brazzi nodded. "That's fair," he said.

"We aren't asking for your blessing," Jack said, "but it does us no good to settle things with Rossetti if the next man in just finishes the job. And you will be the next man in, won't you, Anthony?"

Brazzi said nothing and took a drink.

"Of course, someone would have to answer for what happened," Jack said. "That'd be a swell excuse to wake up the troops that have started to go soft and knock back a rival organization that is getting too big for its britches."

Brazzi nodded so slightly that he might have been unaware that he was doing it.

"The Riverton deal can still go through," Jack said. "We'd never be able to stop it anyway. One proviso: in

*order to avoid suspicion or attracting unwanted attention,
your boys lay off a bar called Spenser's Place. Let the
government buy him out."*

Brazzi was curious. "Why?" he asked.

"He's our client," I said simply.

*"You're an interesting pair, you know that?" Brazzi
said, and then thought for a minute. He tossed back the
last of his drink and made himself another. "It will never
work," he said. "You'd never get near him."*

"Let us worry about that," Jack said.

*Brazzi shook his head. "No," he said. "It would have
to be done just so. If you were seen, if you were identified,
the leg-breakers would hit you on reflex, and Al's money
men would take over. None of us would ever see a dime
from Riverton and the organization would just disappear.
If power is going to shift to a soldier, it has to be done just
so."*

*Brazzi crossed the room to the telephone and picked up
the receiver. I started toward him as he began to dial, but
Jack just shook his head and I kept still.*

*"Al?" Brazzi said after a moment. "Tony. Chick
Mason wants a meet."*

Brazzi listened for a moment.

*"I agree, Al," Brazzi said, "but I think he's ready to
deal. You said it yourself, there are parts of the old
business that we just don't want any more. We may as well
sell the rights rather than just walk away and let it get
carved up. If Mason is smart enough to show a little
respect, I think we have to listen to him."*

Another moment of silence as he listened.

*"That's right. With his temper, if we say no, he could
make a lot of trouble. Trouble that we can't have right
before the Riverton deal goes through."*

Silence.

*"If you say yes, it's all agreed," Brazzi said. "I'll pick
the place and look it over myself. It'll just be you and your*

boys and Mason and that big gorilla of his. Maybe half an hour, tops. Then Mason's number two and I can thrash out details and payment schedules."

Silence.

"All right, Al," Brazzi said. "I'll take care of everything."

He hung up the telephone and turned to look at us.

"The back room at the Rex," Brazzi said. "You know it?"

Jack nodded. "I know it."

"Ten a.m.," Brazzi said. "The room is soundproof, but be as quiet getting in as you were getting in here. There's a service hallway through the fire door that will get you out. Rossetti has two guys that he has with him all the time. One of them is mine."

Jack nodded. "All right," he said and looked at me. I nodded. It was nice to be asked, even if it was slightly after the fact.

Brazzi took a pull on his second drink. "You seem like a pair of clever dicks," he said. "I wonder if you have thought the next steps out already?"

"A letter to the press," I said simply. "Three copies, to three different reporters, left with three different friends to mail in the event of our mysterious demise. The only reason you would have to hit us is so the boys don't find out it was you that set up the old man. If you lead the organization back to glory, in six months no one will give a damn how you got the job, and we won't have a thing on you."

Brazzi looked me up and down again, much more slowly this time.

"She's not bad," he said to Jack.

"She knows," Jack said.

Chapter Twenty-Nine

We were in the back room of the Rex by nine fifteen the next morning, having spent most of the night driving from nowhere in particular to nowhere else. I hoped this worked. I could use some sleep.

Trixie's bit about the three letters had been convincing. Convincing enough that we decided we should actually do something more or less exactly like that. If Brazzi was conning us, if this was a set-up, at least we could hope that he'd lose Rossetti's shirt for him in the process. And afterwards, one may presume his own head. So we wrote out letters full of details, the whole mess, and sealed them up with instructions regarding the aftermath of our grisly demise. It isn't easy to think about who you send something like that to, but we did it. About eleven thirty we had finally posted them from the lobby of the Metrolite Hotel, throwing in some of the better prints from the Jimmy Lish collection for good measure. It was all pretty neat and tidy, except for the grisly demise part which I was still keen to avoid.

Mallick's Coffee House was mostly retail, but he still opened up at eight the morning, and I was back on a nice even keel by the time we made our way into the back room of the Rex Hotel, which was more of a saloon with some rooms to flop located above. The back room was regularly used as a meeting place by less than legitimate businessmen, and the staff had long ago learned to pay no attention to who went in or who came out.

Past the heavy wooden doors were three steps down, each one about six feet wide as if to accommodate the crowds that had used this room when it was a speakeasy. The rest of the room may once have been mostly dance floor, and you could tell where the bar had been from the marks along the wall where it had been removed maybe a decade ago. But now the room was dominated by a conference table, about twelve feet long, with one end pointing toward the stairs. Trixie and I removed all but two seats, one at each end and I stood on the chair opposite the entrance and twisted out the light bulb above that end of the table. Then I sat down, Trixie took up her position behind the door, and we waited.

She was nervous. She'd be damned before she'd show it, but she was nervous. I'd have bet real money that she'd never done anything like this before, but she kept her cool and played her part. She just had less to say than usual, which wasn't a bad thing either. Some people get chatty when they're nervous and can't wait quietly under any circumstances. I've always found the opposite to be the better approach myself, and since she didn't seem to mind, we waited in silence.

The door didn't open until ten past, and those last ten minutes were the worst. We were down to our final trick here, and if we got trumped it was the end of everything. I tried not to think about that by thinking about breakfast instead, which I had not actually had yet and would probably not want afterward.

At last the heavy doors opened and a man the size of a mountain walked in. His eyes were expressionless as he took in the scene. This one had to be Rossetti's. In his day this is what you wanted in a bodyguard. Didn't matter that he was slow and probably thick as a plank. He was the biggest man Rossetti could find, and that meant his boss was important. He stood at the bottom of the steps like a stone colossus and stared at me as I sat in the semi-shadows.

From behind him I heard the click of expensive shoes on the tiled steps. Rossetti was entering slowly, as if the meeting meant nothing to him. He was so deliberately aloof he hardly even looked at the table and didn't seem to register that I was alone.

A third shape came in, carefully closing the doors behind him and locking them from the inside quietly. No reason for him to do that unless he was Brazzi's man.

Rossetti looked up and saw what I sincerely hoped was my shadowy form. He snorted in disgust. "Going for the dramatic effect, Chick?" he asked. It was a good thing he wasn't really meeting Chick Mason today. Mason was known to have a pretty bad temper and probably wouldn't have appreciated the contempt. Of course, I'm not entirely sure how much worse things could have gotten for Rossetti today, but I felt sure that Mason would have found a way. I said nothing.

The man at the door slipped in behind his giant companion, who did not react or move until he suddenly gasped. He twitched one arm three times, as though reaching for an itch in his sleep as his eyes rolled back into his head. He fell forward onto his face like a bag of sand and I knew that he was dead.

"Sorry, Sal," Brazzi's man said quietly, a knife in his hand.

Rossetti stared, his face a mask of wonder.

"Where do you want it?" I asked from where I sat, the room obliging me with an echo like thunder rolling in over the mountains.

The man with the knife shrugged. "Make it convincing," he said. "I got a reputation to keep."

"Joey," Rossetti said, his voice an angry wheeze, "what the hell is this?"

"Sorry, Al," Joey said. "Just business."

"Joey," I said, "take off your hat."

"What?" Joey asked. "Sure thing." He was confused but he obliged, removing his grey fedora just before the sap in Trixie's hand came down on the back of his head. He went limp and fell. Poor guy. He'd feel that for weeks. I know I always did, back in the day when I was earning the name 'Black Jack' by taking a sap from every punk in town.

"Yes?" I asked.

"He'll live," Trixie spat. She was pretty tough, and even Rossetti bought it. But I could tell she couldn't look the old man in the eye.

"What the hell is this, Mason?" Rossetti asked, furious. "You ready for a war?"

"Doesn't matter if he's ready or not," I said. "There's a war coming. My guess is he takes it all though. Your boys are soft."

"You're not Mason," Rossetti said.

"No," I said, "I'm not."

"Well?" he fumed. Big Al was not used to someone else controlling the tempo of the conversation.

"I'm Jack Justice," I said.

"Who?" Rossetti asked.

"That's cute," I said. "I like that. But you're not the soldier that you were fifteen years ago, Rossetti. You don't put out enough death marks these days that you don't know who every one of them is."

"All right, wiseguy," Rossetti said. "You're that dumb private dick that got in the middle of my business." He looked at Trixie. "And this must be Dixon. What, are you two working a sister act these days?"

Trixie said nothing, but she did meet his gaze and held it, hard.

"All right," Rossetti stepped into the room like he was going to take his seat at the table, "you wanted a meeting and you got it."

"That's not why I'm here," I said, standing.

"Don't be stupid," Rossetti said with contempt.

"You killed four people," I said, stepping away from the chair and into the light.

"I've killed a lot more than that," he said.

"Not lately," I said. "And no one you loved like Janet Timms."

"Janet," he almost whispered. "You knew Janet?"

I shook my head. "I only saw her once."

"She belonged to me," Rossetti said as if it were a simple, incontestable fact. "From the time she was sixteen, she was mine. I gave her everything. It took a hell of a nerve for her to betray me."

"Maybe she wanted her life back," I said. "Maybe she felt it was worth more than what you'd paid for it."

"And maybe in the end she was just another parasite," Rossetti said. "Another greedy, grasping whore. You know how many people have their hands out to me every single day? Why should I take that from a used-up moll like Janet? She knew what the Long Branch meant to me."

"So you killed her," I said.

"Yes," he said. "There were millions of dollars at stake. Don't tell me you haven't done it for a hell of a lot less."

I had nothing to say to that, so I didn't.

"Is that it?" Rossetti asked. "Is that the end of your righteousness? She was beautiful and she broke my heart and I killed her. So what? And who else are we supposed to cry over? That piece of trash Jimmy Lish?"

"How about Anne Mayfield?" Trixie said quietly. "She never did a thing to you, you never even met her. You framed her and strung her up like a dog."

Rossetti nodded. "That felt like a mistake," he admitted, as though the words absolved him of any blame. "We thought Mayfield could still be saved. But she had him in a panic, and she wouldn't lay off. Even when my boys tried to put the scare in her, she just wouldn't let it go. She was wronged and she was going to tell the world. We couldn't have that."

"Just business," Trixie said.

"Just business," he agreed. "But Mayfield never would settle down. He kept right on making stupid mistakes. Like he did when he involved you," he said, looking back to me. "That was stupid. When he discovered the photos at Janet's, he should have come right to me. Maybe he didn't trust me. Didn't know for sure that I wasn't behind it all. He'd never have said so, of course. But he was a weak man. Never built for crime, not even a soft one."

"Does what you did to Riverton feel like a soft crime?" I asked.

Rossetti snorted. "Riverton? Are we down to that? Don't you know what they say? The expressway is bringing a new age of prosperity, and it's going right into the heart of Riverton."

"Don't talk politics," I said, "it's beneath you."

Rossetti laughed. "You're right, Justice. The truth is I don't know what the expressway will do and I don't care. I just know that from the time I saw the plans for this, I knew this was the way. Put the money I had worked for all my life, and my father before me, into buildings – sell them to the government at a profit that would more than cover the tax and presto, the Rossettis are legit. No more intrigue, no more meetings in the back room at the Rex. And 'just business' can finally mean exactly that. I worked for this for longer than you could know, Justice. And nothing was going to queer this deal for me."

"Nothing," I said, "but here we are."

Rossetti shrugged. "You made your point," he said. "You want the mark taken off you? It's gone."

Trixie looked at me. I didn't take my eyes off Rossetti.

"Somehow I'm not sure I can believe you, Al," I said dryly.

"I mean it," Rossetti said. "You're smart enough, you're tough enough. I could use you. Both of you. You see I can't trust any of my old crowd." He indicated his fallen bodyguards. "This time next month, Al Rossetti is totally legit and you can get in on the ground floor."

"Trixie?" I asked. I knew what the answer was, but it seemed like the time to ask anyway.

"We should go," she said, breaking away from the spot by the stairs she had held down all this time, making for the door that led to the back hall. If she didn't want to watch, it was okay.

I raised the pistol in my hand. It was a .38. Unfamiliar, but reliable. It would get the job done. My guts were churning. They always did. It didn't matter how many times you'd been here, it didn't matter if it was them or you, it didn't matter how good at it you were. I wondered if Big Al Rossetti knew what I was feeling.

"Wait," Rossetti ordered. "Don't be stupid. We can make a deal."

A man like that kills a lot of people, but he never pulls the trigger himself. He wouldn't have understood.

"Sorry, Al. Just business," I lied. "And we already made a deal with the new management."

Chapter Thirty

I had been packing up my office for about an hour when he pushed open the door. He had a paper bag in his hand and was wearing a suit that was actually more wrinkled than the one he'd had on the day before.

"Wow," Jack said, "this place looks like hell."

"Thanks so much," I snapped. "You really know how to brighten the joint up."

"I mean it," he said. "It didn't look this bad when I left it. I mean, you got rid of the two dead guys, which is probably a good move, but other than that..."

"It was the cops, idiot," I replied. "Rossetti's boys tossed the place looking for my camera, and Sabien's boys tossed it again trying to figure out what they had been looking for."

"They could have just asked us."

"We wouldn't have told them," I said. "We're funny like that."

He thought about this for a minute. "I'm not at all sure that we didn't tell them," he said. "We've spent so much time downtown lately I can't keep it straight."

"Yeah," I agreed, still working. Jack was looking around as though he'd lost something.

"Can I help you?" I asked, testily.

"Where's the coffeepot?" he said.

"Oh, for Pete's sake," I said, throwing the pile of papers in my arms into a box, "I don't keep a coffeepot in the office, Jack."

He seemed baffled by this. "How do you live?" he asked at last, and I'm not sure that he was joking.

"You have a problem, you know that?"

He nodded. "Not just one," he said, "they are legion."

"Do you want a scotch?" I asked, with a pretty good idea of what the answer would be.

"It's ten o'clock in the morning," he said.

"What are you, the speaking clock?" I asked.

"Well," he said, "when you put it that way..."

I opened the desk drawer. The bottle was still in there, but it was dry as a bone.

"Lousy cops," I said in astonishment.

"Now, now," Jack shrugged, "it could have been the mobsters sent to kill you."

"You know it was the cops," I said.

"Yes, it was," he agreed.

"Did you want something?" I asked.

"I did," he said, "but you're out of both coffee and scotch. Don't tell me there's another option."

"There is not," I said.

"Ah," he nodded, gazing at the piles of paper like drifting snow.

"I'm going to try this again," I said, rephrasing the question. "Was there some particular reason that you dropped by?"

"Oh," he said, comprehension dawning on him at long last. He reached into the paper bag and pulled out my camera with the air of one who expected applause.

"Where's the case?" I asked.

"The what?" he said, his face falling.

"The case. For the camera," I growled. "Don't tell me you left it in Samuel Berker's office."

"Who's Samuel Berker?" he asked.

"The Notary," I said through gritted teeth. "Did you leave it there?"

"No, no," Jack seemed mildly embarrassed. "I have it. I just put some stuff down on top of it and kind of... forgot about it. Certain parts of my office kind of look like yours."

"This is not how my office normally looks," I said, picking up more paper and stuffing it into the open bankers' box.

"No, I remember," he said. "Last time I was here you had a couple of dead guys as throw pillows."

"Again with the dead guys," I sighed.

"Yeah," he agreed, holding out my camera at arm's length. *"Where should I put this?"*

I looked at him for a moment. *"True or false,"* I said, *"if I take that back from you as it is, I'll never see the case again."*

"That is not true," he said, trying to seem offended. *"Well, actually, yes it is, but it's also kind of a miracle that I brought this back at all."*

"Give it to me," I said, taking it and setting it down on a clear spot on the desk which I found with some difficulty. *"I want my case back by Monday or I'll hunt you down and kill you like a dog."*

"That's tough, but fair," he declared. *"And in that spirit, you owe me two-fifty."*

"What?" I protested.

"For the Spenser job," he said. *"You pocketed the extra five. You owe me two-fifty."*

"I do not owe you two-fifty," I said. *"I did five dollars more detecting than you."*

"I'm the one that shot everybody."

"You did, didn't you?" I admitted grudgingly.

"And don't think I'm not a little surprised by that," he said.

"I'll get the next round," I shrugged.

"Un-huh," he said. *"Two-fifty."*

"Fine," I sighed. *"Hand me my purse."*

"No need," he said, producing a small pile of bills from his pocket and setting them on a full box on my desk chair. *"I've taken the liberty of extracting it from your share."*

I looked at the money. *"What the hell is that?"* I said.

"Money," he said. *"Tokens of exchange used by many cultures to-"*

"No," I said, mostly ignoring him, *"I mean, what is that?"*

"Fifty-four dollars and eleven cents," he said. "Except I don't have a dime, so I'll have to owe you the eleven cents."

I was getting annoyed. "And the source of this bounty is…"

"The certain very shady publisher that I sold the rest of Jimmy Lish's pictures to last night," he said, pleased with himself.

"You did what with who?" I asked, astonished.

He shrugged.

"You sold dirty pictures to a smut magazine?" I said.

"I'm not sure there is an actual magazine involved," Jack said. "It isn't really my forte, but they weren't exactly sunbathing in those pictures. I believe they are copied and sold as prints."

"You sold dirty pictures of two dead people?" I clarified.

"Well, when you put it that way, it just sounds creepy and wrong," he said. "Janet Timms had certainly been featured in this kind of work before, which is what you get for dating a piece of work like Jimmy Lish. I mostly did it because Roger Mayfield would have been horrified, and he was a jackass."

"He was your client," I said.

"He fired me," Jack said. "And he nearly got me killed just by hiring me. He knew Rossetti was involved from the word 'go', and still he dropped me in the middle of that mess. Besides, your client would have been delighted."

"That's true, actually," I had to admit.

"And the creepy guy I sold them to seemed to think they were worth something to him, and who am I to stand in the way of free enterprise? He paid me, and fifty-four dollars and eleven cents is your share, after I deduct the two-fifty you tried to stiff me on."

I thought about the math for a moment. "He paid you a hundred and ten dollars and sixty-one cents?" I asked. "That seems kind of arbitrary."

"Ah," Jack agreed. "I did not mean to imply that your share was equal to half of the total. Merely that it was your share."

"Ah," I said. "You're the original horse's ass, you know that?"

"So I've been told," he smiled. "You don't want it?"

"Yes I want it," I snapped. "Shut up."

"Ah," he said, "touché."

"This isn't going to queer our deal with Brazzi, is it?" I asked. "I mean, if anyone IDs Mayfield from the pictures?"

"I don't think these things have that kind of circulation," Jack said. "And Roger Mayfield will probably have been forgotten by everyone except Sabien by then. Besides, Tony Brazzi is going to have big enough problems soon. Did you see the reviews?"

I nodded. The evening papers had been full of the supposed gangland slaying of Alphonse Rossetti, notorious mobster. "They seem sure it was a mob hit," I said. "It makes sense, really. More sense than the truth."

"The soldiers are lining up behind Brazzi, right enough," Jack said. "But they're pretty ticked off. From what I hear, the only way Brazzi can keep control is to lead them into a war."

"With the Mason gang?" I asked.

Jack nodded. "Mason will chew them up and spit them out. He's an up-and-comer. Aggressive, organized, aggressive, ruthless and aggressive."

"Yes," I said, "but is he aggressive?"

"In fact, he is," Jack said. "He'll never even bother to deny the Rossetti hit. It's like a Christmas present to him. Brazzi and his boy on the inside are the only ones that

know the truth, and they'll probably both be dead in a month. Maybe less."

"Hap Spenser probably knows the truth," I said.

"Hap Spenser doesn't seem like he'll cry over it," Jack said. "Besides, who's going to listen? Everybody knows that Chick Mason killed Al Rossetti."

I was quiet for a moment. "Think we went too far?" I asked.

"Yes," he nodded. "But it was all we could do except die."

"Maybe," I shrugged, and thought another moment. "I never went that far before," I said at last.

"And I'll bet you can't remember the last time you said that," Jack said with a raised eyebrow.

"Shut up," I smiled in spite of myself. Well, it was true.

"Look, if you feel wrong about it," Jack said, "remember, it wasn't you that did it, it was me."

"That's crap," I said and meant it. "We planned it together and we did it together. And if it was him or me, let it be him, I say."

"What about me?" Jack said, pitching me a softball.

I shrugged. "You could go either way."

"Real nice," he said. "Though I guess that's progress anyway."

"I guess. Listen, I should get back to this."

"Sure," he said. "I'll drop by with the case next week."

"I won't be here." I crammed another armload of paper into an open box. "I'll call you when I'm settled."

"What do you mean?" he asked.

I stared at him for a moment. "Did you really not notice all of the cardboard boxes?"

He looked at them. "I thought you were cleaning."

"I am," I said. "Into boxes."

"Why?" Jack asked.

"My landlord is giving me the heave-ho," I said.

"Because you had a break-in?" Jack asked.

"No, because two people were shot in my office," I said, *"and they were here to shoot me. And then the place was lousy with cops for a day. The other tenants got the heebie-jeebies about the double-murder."*

"Double-murder?" Jack protested.

"His words, not mine," I said.

"That is totally unfair," Jack said. "It was double-manslaughter at best. And besides, I wasn't even charged. They were here to kill you."

"That is also part of his problem with the whole thing, Jack," I said.

"Still," Jack said, "he can't just throw you out."

"I've been late with the rent often enough," I said. "He can pretty much do whatever he wants and he knows it."

"Where are you gonna go?" Jack asked.

I shrugged. "I'll figure something out," I said.

"I'm going to regret this," he said at last, "but there's an empty desk in my office that I never got around to selling."

"I'm not really in the market for a desk, Jack," I said. "I don't have an office to put it in, remember?"

"No," he said, "that isn't what I mean. I mean, you could leave the desk where it is and work there."

I could feel my brow knit in confusion. "Wouldn't it be strange having two detective agencies in the same office?" I asked. "Why wouldn't everyone who walks in the door just come to my desk, on account of I am much less ugly?"

"Because sometimes they are not looking for five-foot ten of bad attitude in a short skirt," he said. "Sometimes they are looking for more of a lantern-jawed thug. Besides, I am not suggesting that we compete. Try not to be dense for a minute, willya?"

"Oh," I said, getting it. "Oh."

"You must get some pretty decent traffic from the ladies with the 'girl detective' routine," he said.

"It's a routine now?" I asked.

"And I do all right myself," he carried on, ignoring me, *"but there are more days when I do nothing than something."*

"And that's 'doing all right', is it?" I asked, although I could say the same and we both knew it.

"I'd bet if we pulled in both crowds, we'd have more than twice as much work," he said. *"And we could keep it at thirty-five a day."*

"Plus expenses," I said.

"The two sweetest words in the English language," he agreed.

"It's a stupid idea," I said.

"Yes, it is," he agreed.

"It'd never work," I said. *"We lived this time, but we're pushing our luck as it is. Besides, I still don't like you."*

"I don't like you either," he agreed. *"But I do hate you less than everybody else."*

"Don't get all mushy on me," I said.

"Never," he agreed.

"Well," I said, *"I guess you're a slightly better option than going out of business and moving back in with my parents."*

"I'm gonna have that printed on some cards," he said with a smile that looked almost genuine.

"All right you big, dumb ape," I said. *"Don't just stand there, help me pack."*

THE END

Á

Printed in Great Britain
by Amazon